THE LEGEND OF THE TAKEN ONES

(Gateskin Chronicles, Book 1)

Janice Spina

PUBLISHED BY JANICE SPINA

COPYRIGHT 2021
JANICE SPINA
Londonderry, New Hampshire

COVER BY JOHN SPINA

ALL RIGHTS RESERVED

ISBN 978-1-7361673-35
(paperback)

LCCN 2021913500

person, please purchase an additional copy for each recipient.

Thank you for respecting the hard work of this author.

ACKNOWLEDGEMENTS

A very special thank you to my wonderful beta readers, Michelle Clement James, Michele Rolfe, John Spina and Frances Stewart for working tirelessly to read and review my work and for their helpful input. Their assistance is invaluable and appreciated.

Thank you to my husband, John, for the beautiful cover and for all the dinners he cooked that made it possible for me to write.

DEDICATION

This fantasy is dedicated to my husband, John, who has been patient enough to read this book about magic and fantasy in which he doesn't always believe. I think at the conclusion of this book he now may be a believer.

For all your support and encouragement, John, I thank you and love you dearly.

To all who believe in fantasy and magic

MAP OF TERRITORY OF NOELLA PROVINCE

CONTENTS

CHARACTERS

Serena Anya (14)   - heroine of
story, sister to Simon and Catalina

Simon Andolferan (12) - brother of
Serena and Catalina

Catalina Leahna (10) - sister of Serena
and Simon

Solinara Queen Fairy - of Sovorotskina
and mother of Serena and siblings

Gateskin - King Wizard of Sovorotskina and father of Serena and Siblings

Sovorotskina - Land of Goodness and Light, home of Serena and Family

Ressaphena   - goddess of Goodness and Light

Ramoforan- god of Goodness and Light

Noella – only surviving child of Sovorotskina, during the capture of Taken Ones   became Queen Fairy of Votovia

Sonovan - 1st King Wizard, husband of   Noella, and ruler of Votovia

Noella II - decendant of Noella only surviving child of Legend of Taken Ones

Josoforan - King of Sovorotskina during capture of Taken Ones

Marolena - Queen Fairy of Sovorotskina during capture of Taken Ones

Hotenfaran   - Wizard, uncle of Serena and siblings, brother of Queen Solinara

Procelina - Fairy, aunt of Serena and siblings

Toleran - citizen guard of Sovorotskina

Miserva - citizen of Sovorotskina and wife of Toleran

Peteran - young son of Toleran & Miserva of Sovorotskina

Amora - Land of Faith and Love

Noderan - elder Amorans subject

Merlina - Land of Magic and Mystery

Merlinans - citizens of Merlina

Merona - Land of Myths and Legends (Named after Fairy Princess Merona captured by EO)

Meronans - citizens of Merona

Votovia - Land of Peace and Harmony

Votovians - peaceful but powerful subjects of Votovia

Savina - Queen Fairy of Votovia, present day ruler

Cavelan - King Wizard of Votovia, present day ruler

Adolphin - son of king and queen of Votovia

Anatonia Noella - daughter of king and queen of Votovia

Soneran - member of King Cavelan's guard

Latoran - member of King Cavelan's guard

Sprites - little tree people who lived in the forests around Sovorotskina and the other villages

Spindle - tree Sprite, friend of Serena's / Head Guard of Sovorotskina

Abason - tree Sprite, father of Spindle, Head Counsel of Sprites

Anabal - tree Sprite, mother of Spindle

Micah - brother of Abason, captured by Evil Ones

Parotovina - Land of Darkness and Evil, home of Evil Ones

Beregina – Fairy Queen of Parotovina

Kaposkaran - Wizard King of Parotovina

Parotovinans - citizens of Parotovina

Quilarena - Goddess of Darkness and Evil

Quilottan - God of Darkness and Evil

Kelleran – Gatekeeper of Parotovina

Mitteran - Head Guard of scouting party of Parotovinans

Leanna - wife of Mitteran

Allonso (Al) - son of Mitteran & Leanna

Tessa- daughter of Mitteran & Leanna

Botular – Eyes & ears of King Kaposkaran (HOH – becomes citizen of Sovorotskina)

Zuri - King of Merlina

Zuleima - Queen of Merlina

Zayleen - daughter of King Zuri/Queen Zuleima

Zukan - son of King Zuri/Queen Zuleima

Zuriann - daughter of King Zuri/Queen Zuleima

EVIL ONES – EOs

TAKEN ONES – TOs

DESCENDANTS OF TOs – Ds

PROLOGUE

At one time the land was known as Territory of Noella Province to honor the first fairy queen who moved from the region of Sovorotskina to the village later known as Votovia. As time passed, the Noella Province separated into the different villages. The elders still called it Noella Province but the younger ones did not, though they were taught the history of the land.

The villages each had their own wizard king and fairy queen who ruled their individual regions.

Sovorotskina – Land of Goodness & Light – ruled by Wizard King Gateskin and Fairy Queen Solinara

Votovia – Land of Magic & Mystery – ruled by Wizard King Cavelan and Fairy Queen Savina

Merona – Land of Peace & Harmony – ruled by Healers (old wise men)

Merlina – Land of Myths & Legends – ruled by Wizard King Zuri and Fairy Queen Zuleima

Amora – Land of Faith & Love – ruled by King Noderan (not a wizard), and Queen Davora (not a fairy)

Parotovina – Land of Evil & Darkness – ruled by Wizard King Kaposkaran and Fairy Queen Beregina

The strongest wizard of all was Gateskin. He ruled Sovorotskina with a firm but kind hand and aided the other villages when needed. He and the ruler of Votovia, King Cavelan, protected the regions from the evil Wizard King Kaposkaran who continued to reap terror upon his own citizens if they did not do his evil deeds.

This king also consistently threatened to harm the other villages.

To the north of the land lay the Unknown Territory. It did not have another name, but it was feared by the villagers. They did not venture over the border. Some who did in the past never returned.

The villagers did not talk about this territory but kept clear of its borders. They did not want to explore, for they were fearful of what was unknown and were content in their own land.

To the south lay the Sea of Shakelle which was a dark and stormy sea that crushed many ships that tried to ride its course. They did not need to travel to the ocean for food since they had plenty from the waterways that coursed through their villages.

If one day they depleted this supply of fish, they may have to look to the Sea of Shakelle for food. The power of the wizards was what kept the villagers secure in their lives and free from worry.

This is where the story begins – one hundred years ago in the village known as Sovorotskina.

A HUNDRED YEARS AGO
Village of Sovorotskina

CHAPTER 1

The land was fertile and green as the sun was rising on this warm, beautiful morning to send its golden rays down onto the Land of Sovorotskina, also known as the Land of Goodness and Light.

People were out in the fields tending to their gardens unaware of what was soon to transpire.

They were the Sovorotskinans, people who lived in peace and harmony with faith and love as their companions. They had been bringing up their families in this way for hundreds of years. They were farmers, butchers, bakers, and wood and stone carvers. They traveled to and from the marketplace to sell and/or trade their produce, animals, baked goods and carvings.

Life had been tranquil until then. If only they had known soon enough, they could have taken refuge and protected their children from the Evil Ones.

The sky had suddenly grown dark as the sound of thunder reverberated over the hills and plains of their land. The Evil Ones had come in swarms of black capes flying across the sky through the village and sweeping everything aside in their wake. Villagers ran helter skelter picking up whatever tools they could use to try to protect themselves and their families. But to no avail, the Evil Ones were too powerful and the tools were ineffective in harming them. Children were snatched out of their parents' arms and taken out of their homes as their parents tried in vain to protect them from the

Evil Ones who whisked the children away never to be seen again.

After the Evil Ones were gone all was quiet except for the sound of wailing and weeping from those families who had lost their children. It seemed that the Evil Ones had taken all of the children except for one, Noella. She had been sleeping in her crib during this tragic time.

Noella's parents had run into their cottage to try to protect their baby but upon reaching her crib found it empty. They became frantic and began to run from room to room trying to find her. But, how would a baby move from her crib?

Thinking that the Evil Ones had taken their daughter, they held each other and were weeping over losing her when they heard Noella's little voice coming from her cradle.

They ran over to Noella's crib to find her smiling up at them. "Oh my God, Noella. You are safe, my sweet!" her father exclaimed.

Noella's mother cried out with relief, "Oh my darling daughter, where did you go? Thank goodness you were not taken. But how?"

They reached down, picked her up and hugged her protectively to their chests, weeping and laughing at the same time. They felt relieved and happy to have found her safe and unharmed. They could not explain what had transpired and why she had not been in her bed when they had looked earlier. They did not ponder on this matter but were happy just to have her safe and sound.

Noella's parents never mentioned what had transpired with their daughter to the other villagers for they would not have believed it either. King Josoforan could be a kind and benevolent ruler but not when it came to those who used magic. They knew their king did not condone magic in his kingdom and might have taken Noella away from them when she was older for fear of Noella being capable of evil magic. The King sent all those subjects who exhibited any magical powers to his dungeon. He feared what he did not understand. He thought that anyone who had powers was somehow connected to the Evil Ones.

The King had experienced a great loss when he was just a little boy due to the magical powers of an evil wizard. This wizard had come into his home and had killed the King's parents with evil magic when his parents would not give the wizard a medallion. This medallion that belonged to the wizard's ancestors was supposedly buried on this property. The wizard had been told that these peasant farmers knew where the medallion was located and that they were protecting it from being taken by the Evil Ones. The medallion was said to have magical powers of its own and would make its owner very powerful indeed.

The wizard finally gave up searching for the medallion but promised, "You have not seen the last of me. I will return one day."

King Josoforan vowed on his parents' grave, "I will always protect my village from the Evil Ones. I will find that medallion one day and destroy it once and for all to keep the evil wizard away."

For many years he had tried in vain to find the medallion so he could destroy it. There would be others also who would come to try to do this too, but in vain.

Noella's parents promised to always protect her from the King and kept her close to them well into their old age. Noella's magical powers were more evident as she grew older. At the age of five she could disappear at will whenever she wanted to play hide and seek from her parents. In her teens she could make objects disappear or she could blend in with her surroundings.

Noella's parents had told her of the dangers of using magic. "Noella, one day we may not be here to protect you. You must go to the southwestern regions of the land (later known as the Village of Votovia). You will be accepted there with your powers and be safe from harm."

After her parents died, Noella went to live in Votovia, noted for its powerful subjects who used magic only for the common good.

Novella vowed to help her fellow villagers. "I will release all those who are imprisoned in the King's dungeon and take them with me to safety." Noella had gone into the dungeon after she blended in with her surroundings. She distracted the guards and stole the keys. Once inside the dungeon she opened the cages and guided the prisoners out of their prison under a protective covering so that the guards wouldn't see them.

Once freed her fellow citizens exclaimed, "We are grateful to you, Noella, and promise to serve you until our dying days."

Noella grew to be very powerful and became the Queen Fairy of the Land of Votovia after marrying the powerful King Wizard Sonovan. Together they ruled Votovia in peace and harmony for many years. Their offspring continued to rule after their deaths.

The story of Noella, only surviving child of the Legend of the Taken Ones, was carried on throughout the generations of her descendants until the present day. Each female descendant was named Noella either as a first name or middle name to carry on the memory of Noella, the 1st.

Anyone who carried her name was revered and thought to have inherited some of Noella's powers.

PRESENT TIME IN SOVOROTSKINA

LAND OF GOODNESS AND LIGHT

CHAPTER 2

"Look at the pretty flowers, Serena Anya. See the butterfly sitting on the flower. She is very pretty too, just like you, my darling." Queen Solinara looked at her beautiful daughter, who was now two, with her cap of golden curls. Serena was growing up so fast, Queen Solinara thought.

Solinara patted her abdomen which was getting larger by the day. A little fist could be felt pushing against her hand as if trying to reach out to its mother. This child would be coming soon; Solinara could feel it.

Solinara turned to look at Serena who was toddling along chasing the butterfly into the brush. Solinara reacted quickly, and reached out to catch Serena before she could go too far.

"Come along, little one. It is time for your lunch and then a nap. I need to rest a little myself. You will soon have a little brother to play with, Serena."

Serena looked at her mother with a smile that caused her eyes to sparkle and dimples to appear at her cheeks. She reached for her mother and climbed up over the bulge of her mother's abdomen to hug Solinara around the neck.

Solinara hugged Serena fiercely in return and inhaled the sweet fragrance of her daughter's skin which was like honeysuckle and roses. Solinara had not experienced anything like motherhood even with all her powers. Nothing could ever come close to this bond she felt with her daughter and the son growing inside her. Solinara knew she would do anything to protect her children.

The Queen looked up at the sky and the bright sun and noticed a dark cloud coming in from the south. It was not a good sign. She hurried along the trail and soon reached their modest cottage in the clearing.

Once Solinara spotted her husband, King Gateskin, chopping wood in the yard and stacking it between the trees she forgot the dread she had been feeling previously. Gateskin wiped the sweat from his brow with his handkerchief and looked up to see Solinara; a broad smile appeared on his tanned and handsome face. His beard, full of beads of perspiration, could be seen glistening in the sunlight. Solinara smiled back at Gateskin feeling warmth spreading through her, filling her with so much love, that she felt she could burst. Gateskin was such a good man and she was a very fortunate woman to have him for a husband. He took great care of her and their daughter.

Serena saw her father and squealed with delight. She struggled in her mother's arms and said, "Dada, dada," in her sweet little voice.

King Gateskin smiled and dropped the axe and ran toward Serena with his arms outstretched. Serena toddled as quickly as her little legs could carry her to her father's strong outstretched arms. Gateskin lifted Serena high and swung her around before pulling her protectively to his chest. He hugged her with such tenderness that Solinara found her eyes misting up and her vision getting blurry from tears of happiness. Serena's face was ecstatic too. Solinara watched as her daughter touched Gateskin's face with her little hand and planted a wet kiss on his nose.

Gateskin kissed her in return and said, "My sweet angel. How are you?"

Solinara babbled, "Dada, dada, I'm hungry."

"Okay, sweet one. Let's get you some lunch."

Solinara felt a kick to her abdomen from her son. It seemed that he was happy to be near his father also. The pain in Solinara's back was stronger now. He must be moving down into position for birth, Solinara thought. I have to get into the cottage and prepare for his coming, she thought urgently.

Solinara caught Gateskin's eye as she stretched and arched her body to alleviate the ache. Gateskin noticed Solinara's discomfort and quickly moved to her side, assisting her to their cottage as he held protectively to both his daughter and wife.

"Are you okay, my love?" Gateskin's face registered deep concern.

"Yes, dear. I just need to get inside. It is almost time."

As soon as they entered the spacious family room and kitchen area, Gateskin put pillows on the large wooden bench and arranged them so his wife could lie down comfortably. He placed a cool, wet cloth on her forehead and put Serena in her chair so he could feed her lunch and then put her down for a nap. He knew his wife would soon need all his attention to deliver their son.

Gateskin had known it was a boy from the second month when he had placed his hands over his wife's abdomen and had received a vision of what the child would look like at birth.

Solinara had requested that Gateskin let her deliver this baby naturally for the safety and health of the baby. She did not want to use any of their powers. Solinara also knew it would not be easy since she had delivered their daughter naturally.

"Remember, Gateskin, I want to deliver this baby without any magic. You promised me to do that."

"Of course, Solinara. I will do that." Gateskin smiled and nodded but had other intentions.

A SON

CHAPTER 3

The pains were coming quickly now and Solinara's breathing became shallower. Gateskin feared for his wife's life and that of the baby's, for she had been in labor for more than seventeen hours now with no sign of the baby coming.

Gateskin rubbed Solinara's shoulders and her lower back as he said, "Let me try to get you more comfortable, my love." Solinara rolled to her side to try to get more comfortable.

Gateskin had since carried Solinara over to their bed which was a lot softer than the padded bench. Their three bedrooms were at the back of the cottage, each separated by a wall. Their room was the largest. Serena had her own smaller room and the third room was to be the baby's room when he was old enough to sleep in his own bed. For the time being the baby would stay in their room.

Gateskin had not been able to sleep much during the night as he lay beside Solinara, waking often to check on her each time she moaned. He had finally gotten up to take care of Serena when he heard her calling him to feed her breakfast early the next morning. After breakfast, Gateskin set up a play area with Serena's toys close by so he could keep a watchful eye on her while he attended to Solinara.

Turning his attention to his wife, Gateskin offered, "Here, Solinara. Try to drink some tea and take a bite of toast to keep up your strength."

He then placed a cool cloth on her forehead. Solinara couldn't eat but took a quick sip of the tea and tried to talk but only a moan came out. "Oh, owww!"

She looked at Gateskin with pain-filled eyes that pleaded with him to help her.

After taking a few more sips of the tea, which Gateskin had laced with some strong herbs to relax and ease her pain, Solinara smiled wanly through the pain at her husband.

She thanked him through gritted teeth, "Thank you, dear, for taking care of me."

Gateskin is one of a kind, she thought. Solinara instinctively rubbed her abdomen tenderly letting the baby know his mother was anxiously waiting for him. Solinara knew in her heart it was a boy even before Gateskin had told her.

The baby pushed down on Solinara causing her to gasp with the wave of pain as it traveled through her abdomen and down into her lower body. The baby was trying desperately to leave her womb to come into this world.

"May the Heavens and all that is holy and good help him!" Solinara exclaimed in silent prayer through clenched teeth.

As she was concentrating on these thoughts, Solinara pushed as hard as she could and sighed heavily, "Ahh, he's coming!" and felt a gush of fluid run down her legs and a release of pressure as the baby was welcomed into his father's waiting arms. After cleaning him off and making sure he was breathing, Gateskin wrapped their son in a soft blanket. The baby did not cry but just gave a great sigh as he entered his new world.

Gateskin handed off his son to Solinara who was exhausted but relieved and happy to take him into her arms.

Solinara looked down at her beautiful son and announced, "He is so beautiful, Gateskin! He will be called, Simon Andolferan, after my father and your father respectively."

Gateskin smiled, his eyes filled with love and approval, as he watched his wife holding their precious son. "Yes, my love, he is beautiful! I like that name. It will honor both our fathers. Thank you, Solinara."

Gateskin couldn't imagine feeling more fulfilled than he was right now with his beautiful wife, daughter and son. Life was complete. He knew he would watch over them with every ounce of his being to ensure they would always be safe.

Simon nestled against his mother looking for food. His mother took care of his needs and before he could finish nursing, he was sound asleep with an angelic and peaceful look on his face.

"Gateskin, look at Simon. He is certainly dreaming of angels and fairies," Solinara sighed.

Serena toddled over to her mother and looked with curiosity at the bundle in her mother's arms. Serena pointed with her little finger at the bundle and said, "Baby."

Solinara turned Simon toward his big sister so she could see his face. "Serena, this is your brother Simon."

Serena smiled broadly, showing her little front teeth, and leaned forward to kiss the silky soft hair on her new little brother's head. Serena excitedly told her mother, "Mama, Serena play with baby?

"Oh, not yet, Serena, Simon is too small and can not walk or play. It will be a little while yet before he can play with you, sweetheart. But you can help Mama take care of him, ok?"

Serena beamed at her mother and patted the blanket that was covering her brother to show that she could help. She toddled over to get a cloth diaper and brought it back to her mother.

Solinara, chuckled and said, "That's a bright girl, Serena; I will need to use that when I change Simon's diaper in a little while. Thank you, sweetie."

Gateskin came over to Serena and scooped her up and swung her around and finally planted a kiss on her round cheek.

Serena giggled when Gateskin's beard tickled her face. "You tickled me, Dada." She then wriggled out of his arms to go play with her toys again.

Gateskin looked with love at his wife and son both sleeping soundly now. He reached over to pick Simon up and put him into the crib that he had made when Serena was born. A month ago, Gateskin had sanded and polished the crib again to take out the dents until it gleamed. Solinara had sewn new sheets and a coverlet in soft shades of blue and yellow with appliqués of animal designs.

Mother and son were both very tired and needed their rest. Gateskin would be there when they woke up (if, and when they needed him).

Gateskin went over to one of the rocking chairs that he had built by the fireplace to sit and finish some of his whittling, toys for his new son, while he kept a close watch over Serena. She was entertaining herself pretending to be mommy to one of her dolls.

Gateskin had also built their cottage and the poster bed, bureaus and night stands. Woodworking was his craft besides farming all their own food. Gateskin sighed, "I have much to do for my family. Thank goodness Solinara didn't have too difficult a time after drinking a little tea. I hope she will forgive me for doing that. If I am lucky, she will not find out."

Both King Gateskin and Queen Solinara had powers they did not speak of to others for their own safety and that of their children. Some people did not believe in fairies and wizards, which is what they were, and feared what they did not understand. King Gateskin and Queen Solinara chose to live their lives as normally as they could without using their powers. King Gateskin farmed, practiced his woodworking and Queen Solinara excelled in preparing their food, sewing all their clothes and other crafts.

They had chosen to build their home a short distance from the village square of Sovorotskina where they could have a safe place to bring up their children. Even though they were the King and Queen of the Land of Goodness and Light, they wanted to live quietly and in solitude as they kept rule over their land and people. King Gateskin would travel back to the Village to check on the people from time to time to make sure everything was in order. The villagers knew they could depend on King Gateskin to keep their land safe and peaceful. If any of the villagers needed their King, they knew where to find him.

But the King and Queen would soon find out that they could no longer keep from using their powers. Unforeseen evil would come once again to the peaceful Land of Goodness and Light. Not only would their home be in jeopardy but also their land, Sovorotskina, they had come to love, would be forever changed.

A DAUGHTER

CHAPTER 4

Two years have passed

Morning dawned as bright and beautiful as each day had always unfurled in the Land of Goodness and Light, also called the Land of Light.

Solinara mused, "If it had not been for the increasingly dark cloud coming in from the south, it would have been an absolutely perfect day." She dismissed it for the time being as she had done in the past.

Solinara was once again with child and due any day now, her abdomen getting heavier and rounder with each passing day. She expressed her feelings, "The baby is not as active now. I feel sure it is a girl. She is getting ready to come. It would be nice to have a sister for Serena and Simon."

Solinara rose early with the sounds of her son waking. Simon was growing quickly, looking more and more like his father and would be as sturdy and strong one day. He was now two years old.

Solinara fed Simon and put him down to play with his toys. Serena, now four, was running around in circles very excitedly waiting for her mother's attention. She wanted to go outside to look for her favorite butterfly.

Solinara picked Serena up, hugged, kissed her, and put her down to play with her toys. Solinara promised Serena, "We will go outside as soon as I finish cleaning up the breakfast dishes."

Gateskin was out tending the garden and collecting all the new vegetables and fruit. He would be coming in shortly with a basket full for Solinara to preserve. There was always something to be done and her days were filled with plenty to do. Preserving their food and caring for their children fulfilled her. Solinara's life was good and she was beyond happy.

As Solinara put the last dish away into the cabinet Gateskin came in with a basket overflowing with all kinds of vegetables and fruit. "We are truly blessed with another good harvest, Solinara. I'm sorry but I know this will take a long time to prepare and preserve all of these for later use."

Solinara looked at Gateskin and with a twinkle of her eye and a swish of her hand she whisked away the vegetables and fruit from him and they were at once washed, cut, cooked, and put into jars before his very eyes. Solinara had just thought of what the preparations were and they were done without any effort on her part. All Solinara had to do now was put the prepared food away in the pantry. "All done, my dear.

With a little magic it is easy," Solinara winked at her husband.

Gateskin smiled at Solinara and she read his thoughts as he was pondering whether Serena witnessed what Solinara had done.

Solinara said, "I don't think she noticed what I did, Gateskin. She is too busy concentrating on playing with her brother, her toys and with her thoughts of butterflies."

"We must be more careful, my love," Gateskin said tenderly to Solinara. He was always concerned about their children. They did not know yet if either of their children were as gifted as they were. These gifts usually appeared around the age of three or four. But Serena had been showing some early evidence of her powers since the age of two. Gateskin and Solinara had both witnessed Serena moving her toys with her mind from one place to another.

"Solinara, did you notice the sky today?" Gateskin changed topics in mid-stream.

"What did you see, Gateskin?" Solinara's voice was showing deep concern as her eyebrows tightly knitted.

"Well, the sky seems to have a darkening in the south and I feel a change in the air. You know how my senses are very strong to the temperature and weather conditions. My hair is standing up on my arms and I don't like the sensation of an impending storm." Gateskin looked uneasy as he said this; his expression changing from calm to consternation.

"Yes, Gateskin, I have been aware of this darkening since the day Simon was born. Then it disappeared but it seems to be coming this way again more quickly now. It could be just a storm hopefully and not something more threatening to our land. I fear for the children if it is the Evil Ones," Solinara stated as she shivered at the thought.

"As you know, Solinara, many generations ago the Evil Ones came to Sovorotskina and other neighboring villages and kidnapped many of their younger inhabitants to use as slaves. These citizens of Sovorotskina never returned. Their families searched for them but were driven back again and again by the Evil Ones. This time was known as the Legend of the Taken Ones."

"Yes, dear. I know all that."

"Sorry, my love. I get carried away about it all. It should never had happened."

"I know, Gateskin but now we must band together this time to ensure that this does not happen again to our land. The Taken Ones were our relatives and those of our fellow Sovorotskinans. It was an unforgivable thing the Evil Ones did. We are much stronger now and we will protect ourselves. We must call a meeting of the other fairies and wizards across our village and the surrounding villages to band together to form a pact. We all have our individual powers that will be more powerful if used collectively," Solinara stated with fervor as her thoughts spread out in all directions feeling for anything that could be coming their way.

"We have promised we would not use our powers to destroy but only for the common good," Gateskin stressed to Solinara with fire in his eyes.

"I know, Gateskin, but we must protect our children. They could be in danger of being taken." Solinara looked at him with fear, tears coming into her eyes.

"Yes, I agree, Solinara."

"You are such a kind and loving man. I know how much you love your family but still want to stay away from using your powers to protect us. We will wait a little longer, but I will keep in touch through my mind with the neighboring fairies and wizards and send my thoughts and fears to them. We may need their help and added protection too." Solinara put her arms around Gateskin and nestled closer to his heart as she listened to its steady beat.

"I will do everything in my power to keep us safe, I promise you, Solinara," Gateskin said this with such determination that his arms tightened around Solinara suddenly, nearly crushing her body to his. Gateskin sometimes would forget how strong he could be when he felt his family was threatened. He was especially concerned because Solinara was due with their third child. Gateskin could feel the baby pressing against him as he held his queen. Gateskin knew, as with their other children, what sex this child would be. He concentrated on the baby and soon could hear her thoughts. She was getting into position and wanted to meet her family this very day.

Solinara suddenly bent forward holding onto her abdomen as she grimaced in pain. Her labor was starting. As Gateskin had done in the past for the other two deliveries, he prepared a comfortable place for her, this time, on the bed. He was hoping it would not be another long labor for her.

The other two took twelve hours for the birth of Serena and seventeen hours to deliver Simon. Gateskin prayed this child would be quicker and easier for Solinara. Simon's delivery had taken a toll on Solinara even though she had never complained. Solinara again insisted, "Gateskin this too must be a natural delivery."

Gateskin nodded but didn't meet his wife's eyes as he responded, "Yes, dear. I will take care of everything."

King Gateskin checked on Serena and Simon to make sure they were occupied with their toys as he continued his preparations for the delivery of their daughter. He placed a cool cloth on Queen Solinara's head that had been dipped into a potion he had prepared that morning of some herbs and flowers that would help her relax and ease her pain unbeknownst to Solinara. Gateskin felt it was necessary this time since she did not drink enough of the herb tea last time to ease her delivery. He had not done this for the other two deliveries but he didn't want to see his wife suffer too long if he could help it. If Gateskin had asked Solinara first she would have told him she didn't need it. He learned to act without her assent for her own good.

Solinara moaned as she shifted her weight and the baby pressed down on her. "She is coming, Gateskin."

Pillows were propped up behind her head and back and Gateskin laid some towels under her. Gateskin had a pot of water warming on the stove and a face cloth to wash the baby and a soft blanket to wrap around her. The crib was ready for the new baby since Simon was sleeping in his own bed now. Everything was in place; it was all up to the baby.

Gateskin whispered, "Come on, little one. It is time for you to meet your family."

After only a couple of hours Solinara starting grunting and pushing and Gateskin got into position to receive his daughter.

Gateskin sighed in relief, "This looks like it is going to be a much quicker delivery, thank goodness, Solinara."

In between the pains and breathing Solinara announced, "Oh, Gateskin, I want our daughter to be named by you."

Gateskin looked up at his wife and smiled broadly. "Well, I always liked the name Catalina Leahna, which is a combination of my mother's and grandmother's names respectively," Gateskin announced very proudly.

Solinara puffed out a breath and said, "Well, then Catalina Leahna it will be."

"Come on little one, we are waiting for you." Gateskin said as he waited to guide his daughter into the world. After a last hard push from Solinara a tiny cry was heard as Gateskin cut the cord, tied it off, and gently placed Catalina Leahna on the waiting towels. Gateskin took the face cloth that he had dipped into the warm water and carefully washed Catalina's face, eyes, nose, mouth and then the rest of her little body. Gateskin put a diaper and a little shirt on his daughter then wrapped Catalina in the soft blanket and placed her in her mother's waiting arms.

Solinara kissed her daughter's soft forehead and breathed in Catalina's sweet fragrant skin at her neck. "My sweet little Catalina. It is so good to meet you."

Catalina snuggled closer to her mother as her mother began to feed her. Catalina was soon sleeping peacefully in her mother's arms tightly wrapped in her new soft pink blanket.

Gateskin cleaned up the bed and area and looked over lovingly at his wife and daughter and let out a contented sigh. "Life is just wonderful with all the blessings that have been bestowed on us, Solinara. I am truly thankful to Ramoforan and Ressaphena, god and goddess of Goodness and Light. I will always do what I can to to protect my family and honor the gods and our village to the best of my ability with or without my powers."

Solinara looked up at Gateskin and smiled. "Yes, we have been blessed, for that I am thankful. I know you will also always keep us safe, Gateskin. For that too, I am grateful."

Serena and Simon were very quiet during this time and Gateskin went over to see what they were doing. They were sitting quietly, heads together. Serena was moving all Simon's wooden soldiers across the floor in formation while Simon was trying to do the same thing with his wooden wagons and horses. Simon was not as successful as Serena was. But it looked like Simon would soon be displaying his own form of magic for them.

When Serena saw her father watching she stopped and looked up at him guiltily. She then quickly lowered her eyes to look at the floor.

"It is all right, sweetheart. I know you have discovered your powers. We must talk about this and how and when you can use them. It is not safe to use them outside of this cottage. Never use them in front of strangers. Promise me, Serena. It is very important that you do what I tell you." Gateskin looked at her, his eyes softening in the glow of the candlelight lamp on the table next to the bench where he just sat down.

"Yes, Papa, I will not use them anywhere but here. I promise." Serena uplifted her eyes to look at her father; the tears in her eyes were like glistening globes balanced there and ready to fall.

"Oh, my darling little girl, please do not cry. It is not that serious that you have to cry. I am not angry with you. I could never be angry with you. I love you more than life itself, my dear one. I am only trying to protect you from others who may not understand your power and may try to hurt you. Do you understand, Serena, what I am telling you? It will be our secret, these magical things you can do, okay, sweetie?" His voice softened to calm her fears and stop the tears.

"Yes Papa, I love you too! I will not move my toys or anything else unless I am here in our cottage. I don't want to get hurt by anyone. Who will hurt me? Do these people live here in our village?" she asked, curiosity getting the better of her, making her fears somewhat dissipate.

"No, sweet child, they do not live here. They live in some other villages nearby and sometimes they come to visit our village. So, you must always be vigilant."

"What is vigi.........gilant, Papa?" Serena asked, trying to sound out the word.

"Vigilant means to always be ready and prepared. That is what we always must be, watchful of others around us," Gateskin explained patiently.

Simon, who was learning to talk by listening to his family, was taking this conversation in. He may not have understood all if it, but he did try to put in his own points by saying, "Papa, I can fly my toys around the room. Will someone hurt me too?" Simon's voice was sweet, still showing his baby-like nature, since he was just two years old. He was going to be a very bright and articulate young man one day. His eyes shown with his growing intellect.

"Can you, my little man? Will you show me what you can do?" Gateskin couldn't keep the pride from sounding in his voice of his son's accomplishments.

"Look at the horse, Papa, he can fly! I can make the wagons fly and the soldiers too! Can you do this too, Papa?" Simon's voice began to rise as his excitement piqued.

"Oh my, you certainly can make things fly. That is just wonderful, Simon. But you must only do this in the cottage and not in front of strangers like I told Serena, okay, my dear son?" Gateskin tried to look sternly at Simon but failed when Simon mirrored his expression. The three of them ended up rolling around on the floor and laughing so loud they woke up both Queen Solinara and Catalina.

"What is that ruckus over there, you three?" Solinara sat up propping the pillows behind her head to get a better look at her family on the floor. Solinara leaned over the baby's crib which was next to her bed and picked up Catalina who was crying softly, making a mewing sound like a cat.

Solinara pulled Catalina toward her and settled her down to nurse. Catalina was soon comfortable and content after being fed and held closely by her mother.

Queen Solinara looked over at Serena and Simon and called them over to her bedside, "Come, Serena and Simon, and meet your sister." The children got up from the floor with their father and rushed over to their mother's bedside.

"Serena and Simon, here is your new sister Catalina. Isn't she sweet? You are going to be responsible to teach her everything you both know so she can be as smart as both of you. Okay? You are now her big sister and big brother." Solinara smiled at her growing children, feeling such love for them.

Solinara watched Serena and Simon as they touched their little sister's tiny hands and face and then leaned over to kiss Catalina on the cheek. Catalina smiled in her sleep and wiggled closer to her mother's chest.

Solinara smiled and said, "Catalina must feel all the love in this room too."

Gateskin stood behind watching his two older children and reached out to stroke his wife's face and placed a soft kiss on her lips. Gateskin then took Catalina from Solinara's arms to lay her down in her crib for a nap so Solinara could take a much-needed nap also.

Peace and tranquility would reign supreme in their lives for ten more years before things changed.

A JOURNEY BEGINS

CHAPTER 5

"Did you hear, Queen Solinara is calling a meeting of all the fairies and wizards? We must travel to Sovorotskina to meet at her cottage tomorrow evening. We will have to take the children with us. They will not be safe if left with others," Queen Savina told the other fairies and wizards in the village of Votovia that bordered the Land of Light. "We also can not leave them alone in case…they come. We escaped them once before. We were more fortunate than the other villages. Our powers kept us safe." King Cavelan, her husband, nodded his assent as he looked around at the other wizards who nodded silently in return.

There were a lot of low murmurs as the group of fairies and wizards finalized their plans. They all agreed it would not be prudent to leave the children and that they would all surely be safer together. So, they covered their village with a protective spell, put their homes in order and gathered their families. They packed up what little belongings they would need for the trip and headed out early this warm morning. They were determined to make their land safe so their children could grow up safely in the village of Votovia, the Land of Peace and Harmony.

The Votovians looked like a swarm of fluttering butterflies as they moved in a sinuous trail. Their colorful cloaks billowed out behind them. The children flew along behind their parents in contrast wearing their brown dresses or jodhpurs and shirts and vests, laughing and playing and enjoying this new adventure. The children, when they reached the age of thirteen, would then wear more colorful cloaks over their clothes as their parents did. It would be a celebration of their coming of age.

There were wagons to hold their belongings and for the oldest and youngest villagers to ride in if they tired from the long journey. The Queen Fairy Savina, and the King Wizard Cavelan, of the village of Votovia, were at the front of the line and had spread their powers of protection over the group to keep everyone in their care protected. This ensured no child would be lost or could wander outside of their curtain of protection. Nothing could penetrate this curtain. The King and Queen could also move the group together quicker without anyone noticing the increased pace as they got closer to Sovorotskina.

The Votovians were a select group. They were made up of mostly fairies and wizards and their families who kept passing down their powers from one generation to the next. These powers varied amongst them but never faltered and only gained and increased in strength as each child grew to reach maturity. They were coveted by the Evil Ones. For, if the Evil Ones were successful in kidnapping some of the Votovian children, the Evil Ones' powers would be increased greatly and would strengthen their lineage.

The Votovians were feared by other villages that did not have fairies and wizards. Most of these neighboring villages feared what they did not understand. In some of the villages if any villagers showed the slightest sign of unusual tendencies toward magic, they were banished from their homes. These banished villagers with powers usually ended up in Votovia where they could live peacefully and raise a family. Votovia welcomed these banished ones to their land and showed the newcomers how to live without powers in their new home.

Votovians had rules, though, that each Votovian had to live by.

Rule#1: Never use your powers to hurt anyone.
Rule#2: Help your fellow villagers out in any way you can.
Rule#3: Always band together for the common good.
Rule#4: Above all, protect the children.
Rule#5: Powers are to be used in emergency situations if agreed upon

only by the governing council with final approval of the King and Queen of Votovia.

The Votovian children were taught these simple rules in Votovian School from the age of four. They used rhymes and simple language so that the youngest children could understand the rules.

We do not use our powers,
To injure, move or hurt even flowers.
We always protect children like thee,
If danger comes, fast we will flee,
And stay together using our powers only in an emergency.

Votovians were all hoping this day would not come when they would have to use their powers. Their powers collectively were so strong they could destroy everyone in their path. They were a peace-loving people, and this did not come easy for them but they would do whatever they had to do to protect their children and the children of their friends in Sovorotskina and any of the other neighboring villages.

PAROTOVINA

LAND OF DARKNESS AND EVIL

CHAPTER 6

King Kaposkaran, ruler of Parotovina, the Land of Darkness and Evil, called all male subjects to the castle square to talk to them.

"We are in need of more male children and adult males. It has been a very long time since we went to the upper northern villages. Our male children keep dying off. We must replenish our race from the outside until we can figure out what is wrong. Our powers are not the same as they once were. Our people are getting older and as they get older their powers seem to be diminishing."

King Kaposkaran continued, "We must regain our strength and increase our armies. The male children we captured long ago grew strong and when they married our people and had children of their own, their unions seemed to strengthen our powers. But now the third generation is weak and needs new blood to be strengthened. We must bring in some new recruits to bolster our strength once again. There are villages up north where there are no fairies and wizards to protect them. They are the most vulnerable there. The children run free in the fields each day to play after school. That is when we must strike. We will go after the weak link which will in turn bring out the strong ones, the Votovians, who will come forward to protect the weak villages. We will be ready for these Votovians and trap them and bring them back to Parotovina to strengthen our lineage."

Queen Beregina gathered the women in her chamber suites and told them the same thing as her husband. "If you want to have healthy, strong grandchildren you must seek husbands of the other villages for your daughters as soon as they reach adult age. Our male children are dying off before they reach the age of fifteen. There is something wrong and we must find a way to preserve our race. We must overpower the upper northern villagers and take their children and adult males to strengthen our families for generations to come. We will kill off anyone that tries to stop us from fulfilling this need."

The Votovian women were frightened of what the Queen had told them. They did not want to take what was not theirs. They wanted to have their own children. Not all the Parotovinans were evil. They also feared for the safety of their husbands who would have to go off to do the King's evil bidding and possibly die in order to follow the orders of King Kaposkaran.

The men, on the other hand, were ready for a fight. They would do whatever they had to do to preserve their way of life and their families even if it meant taking these other children and adolescent males to accomplish this. The men had no other choice, for if they did not do what was requested by the King, they would be put to death along with their own families.

So, the men and women of Parotovina went home to their families to prepare for the upcoming battle. The wives packed their husbands' knapsacks and kissed them goodbye as they watched them head up north to fulfill their promise to the King.

Numerous female children of all ages gathered outside to wave to their fathers. There were very few male children above the age of ten born to true Parotovinans. They were always kept under close watch by their mothers to ensure that they were well fed and taken care of. They were sickly and did not do well in the sun as their sisters did.

The women who were born in this Land of Evil and Darkness weren't all necessarily evil as their ruler. Their parents and grandparents were Parotovinians too. They didn't know any other home. They knew they sometimes felt lost and had to pray. They only knew that when they needed guidance, they prayed to Quilottan and Quilarena, god and goddess of Darkness and Evil for help to bring their husbands back safely and produce healthy male children in their wombs. As they prayed, they looked off into the distance to see the black clouds of their husbands' billowing cloaks as they flew northward up over the hills and mountains. They looked into their husbands' minds to see what their spouses were thinking. The women saw fear in their husbands' thoughts but at the same time determination to complete their objective so the Votovian men could return to their families.

CHAPTER 7

King Gateskin felt his skin prickling and knew there would soon be visitors at his door. He could feel the change in the air and hear the sounds of voices in the distance long before they would arrive.

King Gateskin prepared his children for the coming of the visitors. "You must be on your best behavior. The Votovians are our friends and are magical people. It will be okay for you to use their powers in front of our guests."

He spoke softly to Queen Solinara about what they would be discussing once their visitors arrived so as not to frighten the children. "We cannot tell our children the real reason the visitors were coming to see us."

The children were excited, not knowing what to expect. All they knew was they would have a lot of adults coming to visit along with many children. The fact they would have many other children to play with, was the most interesting and exciting concept for them. They did not see many other people where they lived. They lived out in the woods of their village and not many people ventured that way.

Queen Solinara was busy in the kitchen using her many powers to prepare the food and drink for her numerous guests. She did not know yet how many were coming.

King Gateskin promised, "Solinara I will give you an estimate as soon as I can count in my head. The Votovians will be tired and hungry after their long journey. Our guests will have much to discuss once they arrive too."

Queen Solinara got the children fed and settled in their very best clothes to make a good impression. She then cleaned herself up and dressed in her best dress and shawl while King Gateskin put the finishing touches on his yard and then to his own garments. Queen Solinara put her long blonde hair up with pins and a little magic. Now they were ready.

King Gateskin had built a large extension onto their cottage for all their guests with plenty of beds and bathroom facilities and tables for dining. He had connected this extension by large double doors to their cottage. Of course, he had to do all this with a bit of magic. He had estimated now how many would be arriving and he was always right on the mark when it came to his estimations.

There was a knock on the door, and they stepped forward together excitedly as a family to answer it. Standing on the stone threshold were over 100 Votovians in colorful hooded cloaks. At the front of the group were King Cavelin and Queen Savina and their two children followed by the council members and then all their families. The eldest Votovians sat in the wagons resting from their long journey as the youngest children at the very end of the group romped and played together.

King Gateskin cleared his throat and extended his hand to King Cavelin and Queen Savina, "Welcome to our humble cottage."

Queen Solinara took Queen Savina aside and hugged her and escorted her into the cottage to show off her children. She stated, "It has been many years since we have seen each other, Queen Savina. We have a lot of catching up to do."

"Yes, Queen Solinara. We certainly do. It is so kind of you to invite us and welcome us to your home."

Queen Savina oohed and aahed over Serena, 14 and Simon, 12 and the youngest child, Catalina who was now 10 years old. "They have grown so tall and beautiful and handsome."

"Thank you, Queen Savina. So are yours," Queen Solinara stated as she gazed at the children.

Queen Savina introduced her children. "This is, Adolphin Raminar, who is 16, and Anatonia Noella is 15." Queen Savina smiled and said, "I cannot have any more children, but I am content to wait for grandchildren one day," she added with a titter.

Queen Solinara, smiled at Savina's remark. "I also will not have any more children. Three is quite enough for me. They are my joys in life though. I too look forward to having grandchildren – many years in the future."

Queen Solinara wanted very much to ask Savina about the middle name of her daughter, Noella. This had to mean she was a descendant of Noella I, from the Legend of the Taken Ones. She thought it would not been the right time to ask, but would ask at another time when they were alone.

The group solemnly followed their King and Queen into the cottage and moved around fluidly. The double doors of the extension were now opened as more and more Votovians filed into the large room. The adults looked around the immense room and went over to pick out beds for their families and a place to put their belongings. King Gateskin had put hooks on the walls and added built in closets for each family to hang their clothes and store their possessions.

The children were told, "Please walk and don't run into the large room."

There were so many children now. They were, surprisingly, not at all tired or at a loss for words. The children looked around at their surroundings and spotted Serena and Simon and Catalina standing there looking at them with wide curious eyes.

Serena and Simon watched the three dozen or so children stream into their cottage and head for their toys. They stood protectively over their play area as the children sized one another up. The boys went over to meet Simon, while the girls went over to Serena. There were girls ranging from age 15 down to two and the boys ranged from age 16 down to three years old. They were all curious about each other and not a bit shy.

The younger children were soon all playing together in the toy area sitting on the large braided rug with the toys. The boys were showing off all their tricks and powers to each other with the wooden soldiers, wagons and horses while the girls played with the wooden dolls, stroller and crib and glass butterflies. The older children gathered together and chatted about their lives and what they planned to do once they were on their own.

King Gateskin had made all the toys for his children spending many long nights carving each item or using his glass blower to shape each intricate butterfly. King Gateskin did not use any of his powers, just a lot of love and his innate skill, with which to produce the toys.

After settling in, the Votovian men sat at the tables and made themselves at home while the women busied themselves with putting things in order for their husbands and children.

Queen Solinara thanked the Votovian women, "I appreciate your kind help with the preparations. Let's check on the children and see if they are getting long."

The two queens stood looking over the children all busily having fun, playing with the toys and getting to know one another better.

Queen Savina said, "I guess we didn't have to worry about them. They are getting along well and having a good time."

Queen Solinara, with the help of Queen Savina and the other women, prepared a meal for the children and got them all settled down for the night. It had been a long journey and the children needed to get some rest.

The adults would be given some refreshments thereafter, and then the Votovian men and King Gateskin would have a serious meeting and discuss their plans. These plans would be long and involved and take most of the night to finalize. But afterward everyone would know what he or she had to do in order to protect their families and each other.

A WARNING

CHAPTER 8

The following day Queen Solinara was already up with the sun and busily preparing breakfast in the kitchen. Queen Solinara wanted to make sure her husband and his companions were fed before they left for their journey, so she had prepared them a large breakfast.

King Gateskin kissed his wife's cheek and exclaimed, "Thank you, sweetheart, for the delicious breakfast. It was just what we all needed."

The rest of the group murmured their thanks too around the table after Queen Savina and King Cavelin announced, "We are indebted to our hosts for this delicious repast. Thank you both so much. We are full to bursting."

Queen Solinara replied, "You are most welcome. But I cannot take full credit for this meal. Queen Savina and all the women here helped me put this together. I thank them in return."

The Votovian women chorused and bowed to Queen Solinara, "You are welcome. It was our pleasure to help."

King Gateskin, after finishing up this breakfast, with the aid of King Cavelin, chose two Votovian guards to accompany him on his visit to his subjects of the Land of Light, Sovorotskina.

King Cavelin took great pride in his men and told King Gateskin the men who were chosen were his personal guards. "These are my most trusted men. I trust them with my life and yours also."

"I can't thank you enough, King Cavelin. We will surely need their assistance in everything that we need to do."

Gateskin explained, "I do not have guards nearby but often use some of the citizens of the village when needed. I keep my men scattered in the village. They are ready for the call from me whenever that may be. I feel I can protect fellow villagers better that way."

"I see. That is a good idea. But you should have some nearby your cottage just in case."

"Yes, I agree. I may do that sooner rather than later. Thank you for your suggestion."

***

The journey was not a long distance but King Gateskin and the Votovian men had hurried on their way just the same to warn the people of the impending danger. There was a lot to be done to ensure the safety of the villagers.

Back at the cottage the children were up and already resuming their activities of the previous day. They were all becoming good friends now and unaware of the impending dangers.

The Votovian women, who enjoyed work, did all the necessary work without the help of their powers. They cleaned up the large room and made up the beds and swept their areas. Once the men were fed, they were sent out to the yard to chop and stack wood for cooking and heating the now larger dwelling. There was plenty for everyone to do. The children were taught to pick up their toys after playing and never to drop food on the floor in order to keep away mice and rats and insects.

Queen Solinara looked around and smiled at the area which was now clean and orderly. She always liked peace, quiet and order and this was difficult for her to have so many people around her other than her immediate family. But the Votovians were an orderly people and were helpful and instinctive in knowing what needed to be done, for this she was grateful.

She walked around and thanked each one in turn, "Everything looks pristine. I thank you for keeping my home looking perfect."

The Votovian woman smiled and bowed as Queen Solinara passed through the extension back to her own rooms.

CHAPTER 9

"Papa, Mama, there are three men coming down the road toward our cottage," Peteran exclaimed to his parents who were busily working in the garden behind their home.

"Peteran, go quickly into the house and do not come out until we say so. Hurry now." Meserva exchanged a wary look with her husband, Toleran, and took the vegetables she had just picked. Taking Peteran by the hand, since he had not yet moved, she led her son into the safety of their house. Toleran walked out to the road to meet the three men.

As Toleran got closer he noticed it was King Gateskin and two other men whom he did not know. He rushed over to greet the King bowing in front of him.

"Oh, sorry, King Gateskin. I did not realize at first it was you. I do not know these men with you."

"Toleran, it is not necessary for you to bow in front of me. I am a king only in the villagers' eyes. I don't think of myself that way at all. I am a citizen just as you are of our beautiful land of Sovorotskina," King Gateskin stated with a kindly expression in his eyes feeling somewhat flattered at the same time at his fellow Sovorotskinan's fervent attentions. He always wanted his fellow villagers to feel equal to him.

"Oh, my King, you are more than that to us. You are our guardian and most precious to us. You are our king and always will be until ..." Toleran bowed again and waited to hear what King Gateskin had to say.

"Thank you, my good man. You are my most honored guard in the village. With your help I will be able to keep you safe, I promise, until I can not do that anymore."

Toleran nodded and waited for more. "It is my pleasure to serve you, my King."

The King smiled and continued, "We are here to meet with the whole village to inform you of the danger that is nearby. Please call the rest of the men to the square so we can talk to them. These two men are Votovians and are here to help all of us protect our families from the dangers coming our way."

"Of course, your Highness, I will go right away to sound the call." Toleran hurried to the square to ring the bell to call all citizens to meet.

King Gateskin and the two Votovian guards, Soneran and Latoran moved quickly to the square as all the citizens of Sovorotskina flooded into the area and stood all around them, a questioning look in their eyes. Some looked fearful.

King Gateskin moved to step up onto the small stone platform in the middle of the square which was used for speakers to address the crowds. He looked around him and assessed the men in the crowd. There were many who were older with a smattering of adolescent males amongst them. There were many stronger men who he had used as his guards in the past. They would help him keep the village safe with their strength and courage.

The adolescents did not look like they were experienced enough to fight, and the elder men were too weak to do anything. King Gateskin feared for his village's safety. He looked at the stronger men and nodded for them to heed his words. He felt somewhat relieved to know the Votovians were here with him to help defend his land and its subjects.

"My fellow citizens of Sovorotskina," King Gateskin began, "I have come to warn you of the dangers that are coming our way from the south," he paused to let them take this in.

"It seems that the Evil Ones of Parotovina are heading this way once again to take what is not theirs. As you all know about the Legend of the Taken Ones, passed down through generations from your relatives from over 100 years ago, when the Evil Ones kidnapped the children, and took them back to their land. We can not let this happen again."

"We know the Evil Ones have already swept through the neighboring villages below us and were not successful in securing any children from those villages. I warned them through their wizards to gather the children and send them to a safe place. I tell you now, my good citizens, to do the same."

"Send your wives and children to the caves in Mt Ailylene with enough food and supplies to last a week and I will send my chosen guards to guard the entrances there. You can not waste time, go home and secure your families safely away. Then you must return here so you can learn to protect yourselves from the wrath of the Parotovinan's when they arrive. The Evil Ones will be enraged when they find no children here."

"I am going to protect you with the help of our friends of Votovia. This man to my left is Latoran and on my right is Soneran. They will stay here with you long enough to prepare all the able-bodied men to defend themselves against the Evil Ones."

At first a loud rumbling from the men was heard as they looked at one another with fear and anger. Then they let out in unison a cry of acceptance and determination as they ran towards their homes to collect their families to send them to the caves as their King had instructed.

King Gateskin waved his arms and felt the air around him and then shivered. He felt that the Evil Ones were closer now. They would arrive before the next sunrise. He put a spell on the trees surrounding the village so that this Fence Enchantment Spell, connecting the trees together like a fence, would keep the Evil Ones out as long as possible. The Evil Ones had their own sorcerers, wizards and witches who had great powers to break this spell but he had to try just the same to deter their advance. He prepared other spells and placed them at different points along the trails in the woods and on the road leading into the village. King Gateskin would do everything in his power to save his fellow citizens of his much beloved Land of Light, Sovorotskina.

The Votovian guards would be using their powers also to keep the women and children safely hidden in the caves of Mt. Ailylene with the Invisibility Curtain Spell placed all around the caves and surrounding areas. Once this was done, the guards would come back into the square and instruct the citizens on hand-to-hand combat in case it came to that. The guards would enchant all the weapons, without the citizens' knowledge, to help protect them against the onslaught of the Evil Ones. After the Votovian guards could ensure the citizens were well protected, they would go to the other surrounding villages to do the same then return to King Gateskin's home to prepare for what would lay ahead for them all if they could not hold off the Evil Ones.

For, King Gateskin knew that the Evil Ones would not stop at anything to get what they wanted.

CHAPTER 10

Queen Solinara and her guests, the Votovians, were all busily preparing the cottage and guest house for the return of her husband and the two Votovian guards. Queen Solinara and the Votovian women had put the Fence Enchantment Spell all around the woods surrounding the building to provide them with notice if anyone was approaching. The surrounding trees would actually turn a brilliant red if anyone approached within 100 yards of either the land or building.

Queen Solinara would know when King Gateskin was near for he would send his thoughts to her. Once King Gateskin and the guards were within a few yards, Queen Solinara would open the invisible boundary that she had created to allow their entrance. Afterward, the opening would close tightly protecting them once again from anyone else entering.

This Tree Enchantment was quite strong since it was the combined efforts of all the fairies' powers and would be unbreakable even by the Evil Ones. The only way it could be opened would be if all of the fairies working together broke it or just Queen Solinara, since this enchantment was her design. If all of them died then the barrier would be broken automatically.

Queen Solinara and the Votovian women were very protective of their children. Queen Solinara ensured them and said, "We are well protected now. The borders are safe and unpenetrable. The Parotovinans will not be able to break through."

They knew their collective spell was unbreakable for as long as they needed it. "Yes,

I agree, Queen Solinara," Queen Savina stated as her fellow Votovians nodded in agreement.

A prickling sensation running through Queen Solinara suddenly got stronger and King Gateskin's thoughts entered her mind as he was nearing the boundary of the enchantment. "Solinara, we are back. Please open up the border."

She looked out and saw the trees turning a brilliant red in the area of the woods where he was approaching. She spread out her fingers and pointed at this area and the trees seemed to disappear at this spot causing a hole to open up in the woods. King Gateskin and the two guards appeared and walked through the hole which closed behind them immediately and the trees reappeared once the red glow faded.

Queen Solinara and the guard's wives ran out to meet their husbands and embraced them with relief. She whispered to Gateskin, "I am relieved that you are back safely, my love. I worried just the same. At least I can see our borders are impenetrable even for you."

Gateskin winked at his wife and said, "Of course, how could I open it if you were the one who closed it so well?"

They all knew how strong their husbands' powers were but still worried about their safety. They also knew how powerful the Evil Ones were and how relentless they could be when they met with any resistance over obtaining their objectives. There were many in the past who had not survived when they tried to fight to protect themselves and their families. Queen Solinara and the Votovian women had to ensure this did not happen to them.

Queen Solinara asked, as she smiled lovingly at her husband, "King Gateskin, do you think the citizens of Sovorotskina will be safe from harm now? Did you use the Fence Enchantment Spell like the one we used here around the perimeter? What about the Invisibility Curtain Spell to protect the women and children?"

King Gateskin chortled as he replied, "Yes my dear, Queen Solinara. We took care of everything. The citizens should be quite safe. We even enchanted their weapons to protect them in case the Evil Ones got that close to the villagers. We will also keep in contact with them through the enchantment over the weapons." King Gateskin smiled back at his lovely wife, giving her another hug.

"How are all the children doing? Did you protect them with the charm I left for you?" he asked anxiously.

"Oh yes, all the Votovian women added their powers to mine and we made it quite strong indeed to protectively cover the children no matter where they played in/or around the house," Queen Solinara added with more emphasis to allay his fears. As you may have noticed, we combined our powers to make the Fence Enchantment Spell as strong as possible and unbreakable."

"Please forgive me, Queen Solinara. I trust your powers and judgment implicitly, my dear wife. You know that. Our children are so very precious to us." King Gateskin looked away in the distance as his eyes misted over.

King Gateskin was just an old softy when it came to his children. Solinara smiled as she watched Gateskin, feeling so proud and happy to have him for a husband and the father of her children.

Queen Solinara's reverie ended when she heard the innocent laughter of the children as they came running and skipping into the room. The children abruptly stopped when they saw their father and mother standing there watching them with somber expressions on their faces.

"Papa, you are home. We missed you," Catalina said as she smiled sweetly at her father and then jumped onto his back begging for a horsey ride with Serena and Simon running along each side of them.

King Gateskin and the children went off galloping around the room and then outside. Catalina's whoops and hollers could be heard echoing around the yard causing Queen Solinara to giggle out loud. Even though Catalina was now ten she never tired of the ride and being close to her father.

Gateskin laughed along with the children and loved every minute of closeness with them. He knew it wouldn't be long before they wouldn't need him as much.

As Queen Solinara watched them, she remembered back to the time she had gone into Catalina's room when she was nearly a year old. Catalina was playing in her crib with her enchanted fairy mobile.

She had been such a sweet little baby and was growing bigger each day. She was the biggest baby Queen Solinara had delivered; luckily, she wasn't the first born. Catalina would surely have been the last, for Solinara's deliveries had been very difficult the first two times. Solinara also knew Gateskin had given her some potion at that time for the pain that relaxed her to aid in the delivery but she never let on to Gateskin she knew. Solinara knew her husband only did it to ease her pain and make her delivery less stressful for her and their baby. She was grateful to Gateskin and this only made her love him more.

Solinara had watched Catalina from the doorway as she reached her little hands up to the mobile of fairies as they flew around in a circle with their wings sparkling with fairy magic. Queen Solinara's breath caught in her chest when she realized Catalina was moving the fairies with her own hands magically in the opposite direction than Solinara had enchanted them to move. Catalina also had a toy in her hand but her hand was not there – it suddenly blended in with the toy changing to the same color and texture as the toy.

Solinara couldn't believe what she was seeing. The other children did not develop or demonstrate their powers until age three or older. Catalina's powers would indeed be very advanced by the time she was two. Queen Solinara decided at that moment she would encourage her children and nurture their powers with her own to strengthen them.

There would come a time when Solinara may not be with them and they would need to be dependent solely upon themselves. She didn't want to even think about that yet.

Life at that moment had been so peaceful, Solinara thought. She hoped her children would always feel peace in their lives and be safe from harm. Mothers sometimes wished for things even a fairy couldn't bring to fruition.

Solinara watched her children playing and running after their father and felt she would enjoy the peace and serenity at the moment and not worry about the future. The future would bring much danger for her children. Solinara just hadn't seen too far into the future to realize it yet.

THE EVIL RULERS

CHAPTER 11

"I invoke the names of Quilarena and Quillotan, god and goddess of the Land of Darkness. Hear my plea as the king of this land. I am sending my men out into the northern villages to take what we need to survive. Help us in our need so that our heritage will prevail. Guide my men on their journey and ensure their success." King Kaposkaran bowed his head beneath the massive stone statues.

King Kaposkaran knelt by the likenesses of the god and goddess of evil in one of the private chambers in his castle. He had many hiding places, tunnels and secret passageways in his private chambers that he could retreat to if he felt his life was threatened or in danger. His queen, Beregina, had her own secret places to go to and they all led to the same place, the King's Garden, where they would meet if the need arose for them to get away.

The King was not a gracious, kind or forgiving ruler to his people. If his subjects did not do his bidding, they were hung in the village square for all to see. He ensured that all of his subjects would bow down to him and no one would go against his wishes. If they did...they would not live to tell anyone.

THE DESCENDANTS OF THE TAKEN ONES

CHAPTER 12

The people in Parotovina were generally good people who were controlled by their evil ruler. Many of them were descendents of those who had been taken from other villages. They knew the story passed down to them from their ancestors. They never lost sight of the fact that they did not belong here and hoped one day to return to their original lands. They never would give up their right to freedom and to bring up their children in peace and harmony.

The men worked hard in the fields tending the King's gardens and the women cleaned the castle and all of its thirty rooms for the Queen. Some of them were cooks and others were chambermaids or personal aides to the Queen.

The most attractive men and women were taken to marry other Votovian citizens to produce more offspring to increase their numbers. If any one of the Taken Ones showed any powers, they were brought before the King or Queen and used to control the people or foresee the future. The Taken Ones were careful thereafter how they used their powers doing everything manually no matter how difficult or tedious their duties were.

These unfortunate citizens had watched as the King's guards flew off to the northern lands to bring others to this evil land. They were descendants of the peoples of the northern lands of Merlina, Amora, Votovia, Merona, and Sovorotskina. They were descendants of those who were taken one hundred years ago from their homes.

Some of these descendants prayed to the god and goddess of Goodness and Light, Ressaphena and Ramoforan, as their descendants of Sovorotskina, the Land of Light, had taught them to stop the evil King's guards from being successful.

It had worked other times in the past and they hoped it would work again this time. These descendants of the Taken Ones truly believed one day they would all be rescued by the people of their lands. They had waited a long time but never would give up. This belief was instilled in them by those who came before them on their deathbeds. Their words were written on a scroll. The scroll was handed down from generation to generation and was kept in an air-tight container with a little magic thrown in to keep the scroll from crumbling. It read:

Never give up,
The Evil Ones you must deceive,
Your wishes will be fulfilled in time,
If only you believe.
Do not let evil rule,
Or break your will,
Stay strong.

Do not be a fool.
Evil will not win over what is good.
Right will come out of wrong.
Life will be peaceful and harmonious as it
should (be).
And all peoples will once again be free.

This creed kept these descendants going and they stayed true to it, sharing it with one another and passing it onto their children in their wills when they died. They never gave up hope that they would once again be free. Even though these descendants were from different northern lands they banded together as one people against the Evil Ones.

They would wait for a sign from the gods that it was time for them to leave. Others had come in the past to rescue them but failed, killed before they could reach the Land of Darkness and Evil. The descendants of the Taken Ones would be ready this time to do whatever it took, even using their own powers, to enable the rescuers to succeed.

THE EVIL ONES RETURN TO

VILLAGE OF AMORA

CHAPTER 13

Amora bordered Parotovina on the south, Merlina and Merona to the west and Sovorotskina to the north. Since Amorans were so close to Parotovina they had to stay alert at all times with the help of their neighbors and King Gateskin.

Amorans were resilient people and had to be prepared at all times for flooding in their village since the Gateskin River ran through it with other tributaries that often overflowed onto their land.

The sky darkened as the black capes of the Evil Ones blotted out the light from the sun as they flew over the land. People of Amora, Land of Faith and Love, were frightened and ran to their homes to arm themselves for the fight ahead using their weapons which had been enchanted by King Gateskin and the Votovian guards.

The women and children were safely tucked away in the caves that were created by the Votovian guards and protected by the Invisibility Curtain Spell that the guards had placed in each village they had visited. In the past the Amorans had feared the magic some had displayed but now they embraced this magic to protect themselves and their families.

The Evil Ones swooped down but could not penetrate the Fence Enchantment Spell that protected the Amorans from above and surrounded them on all four sides of their village. The sorcerers in the group tried every trick that they had to try to break through the Fence Enchantment Spell; nothing worked.

The Amorans cheered as they watched the failed efforts of the Evil Ones. The villagers went back to their homes to wait for any word from the Votovian guards or King Gateskin of Sovorotskina on what they would do if the Parotovinans did manage to break through.

The Amorans kept their enchanted weapons close by. They were told by King Gateskin, "I will get a message to you through your weapons if there is a weakness detected in the Fence Enchantment Spell or the Invisibililty Curtain Spell. Also, you can contact me by looking into your weapons and tapping them three times. I will send messages into your minds through the weapons but you must concentrate and keep your minds open for this to be successful."

These Amorans were common people and not fairies, wizards or witches. Because of the Amoran's fear of the Evil Ones, they concentrated with all their being so they could receive the messages from King Gateskin.

The black-caped invaders kept up their flight back and forth above the Fence Enchantment Spell perimeter trying to find a way in. The Evil Ones were not completely tireless even though they were known to do this for days with only a short rest in between. Some of the most powerful invaders took turns trying different spells on the enchanted area while the others rested. The Evil Ones knew they could not go back to tell their King that they had been unsuccessful. They would all be put to death.

The Head Guard of the Evil Ones sent a message to his men, "We must desist for a short time. Their defences are too strong. Pull back and rest until I tell you to begin again."

The men turned toward their leader and nodded and sent their thoughts to him, "We will do your bidding and wait for word to continue."

The next morning the Amorans, who had slept fitfully all night for fear of the Evil Ones' success, arose and went out of their homes. The villagers looked up at the sky and could now see the sun and how bright it was. There were no black capes flying above. The Evil Ones had left!

There was rejoicing in the streets. The Evils Ones were defeated. The Amorans were all safe for now.

One Amoran, Noderan, had not come out of his hut but had stayed behind to check his enchanted weapon for any message from King Gateskin. He knocked three times on the weapon and cleared his mind and waited.

Noderan closed his eyes, concentrated, and saw a picture in his mind of the black capes flying away from his village to go to the next village of Merlina, Land of Myths and Legends. Noderan could hear King Gateskin's voice telling him, "Go to the people and allay their fears that all is well for now. I will contact you again when it is safe to move the women and children back to their houses."

"Thank you, King Gateskin, for all your help. We are indebted to you," Noderan expressed his thanks to the King.

The Evil Ones were on their way to Merlina. The people of this village had some powers and were using them. They looked like they could take care of themselves along with the spells that King Gateskin had put all around their boundaries. After all, King Gateskin was also watching over them and would ensure the safety of the Merlinans at all costs.

Noderan left his hut and walked outside to see his fellow Amorans celebrating their victory. He went to the center of the square and stepped up on the stone platform and raised his hands to get everyone's attention. Noderan was one of the elder and wise statesmen of his village and was respected by all. Upon seeing him, all citizens quieted down so they could listen to what Noderan had to say.

"My fellow citizens of Amora, I have spoken to King Gateskin of Sovorotskina or should I say he has sent his thoughts to me. He said we are safe for now but we must not let our guard down. King Gateskin also said that the Evil Ones are now in the neighboring village of Merlina. They are not having any success there either."

Noderan continued, "The Evil Ones are becoming very angry because they know they can not return to their land of Parotovina without more Taken Ones. They may return to our village to try again. Please be vigilant and do not move the women and children yet until King Gateskin tells us that they are safe to return."

Noderan saw the shock on the faces of his fellow Amorans. He knew they did not believe the Evil Ones would come back, but they would do as Noderan told them because he was wiser than they. Noderan did not know how long he could convince his fellow citizens to listen to him, though, and hoped King Gateskin would send word soon that all was well.

Before the Amorans dispersed, one citizen stepped forward and announced, "I think we should have an official leader. I nominate Noderan as our leader and king."

There were several ayes and Noderan bowed in thanks, accepted his new post and requested all to return to their homes as instructed to wait for a message from King Gateskin who promised to always help the surrounding villages that did not have a ruler to aid them.

Noderan went back to his home and contacted King Gateskin to announce his new role. "I am honored to be chosen to lead my people as their king. I will do all I can to keep them safe with your continued help, King Gateskin."

Gateskin congratulated Noderan, "You are most deserving of this honor, King Noderan. I am honored to work with and assist you in any way in protecting your village."

Noderan replied, "Thank you, King Gateskin. It would be my honor to work with you to keep my village safe."

He went to his family to announce his new position. They would rejoice with the news but also fear what responsibilities this new position entailed.

His wife hugged him and whispered, "Be careful, my husband. This position does have its rewards but with these rewards comes great responsibility and danger."

"Yes, Davora. I know the dangers. But do you realize that if I am the king of this great village then you are its queen!" Noderan grasped his wife's hand and kissed it in reverence to her new position.

Davora stared in awe and apprehension of what this meant. She exclaimed in a shocked tone, "What is expected of me, Noderan? What must I do?"

"You and I will build a larger home to house my men who will be guards of our great land. We will have much to do, my queen."

VILLAGE OF MERONA

CHAPTER 14

The village of Merona is lush and green from the waters that flowed through the village from Gateskin River. They had built up the banks to keep the water from overflowing into their village. They had plenty of fishing and swimming in the pools that formed around the village.

The skies were dark and menacing over Merona which was bordered by Amora to the east, Parotovina to the south, Merlina and Votovia to the west and Sovorotskina to the north. The male Meronans were huddled inside their huts while their women and children were safely tucked away in the caves of Mt. Harmony cloaked in the enchantment sent by King Gateskin.

Most of the Meronans had never met the King of Sovorotskina but all of them knew of his reputation for being a wise and benevolent ruler. They knew King Gateskin would protect them and their families. He would never leave them to fight alone.

King Gateskin had sent the Votovian guards, Soneran and Lateran, to all the neighboring villages to put enchantments on the villagers' weapons and safely tuck away the women and children. The Meronans now awaited word from him that all was safe for them, as did each village, before venturing out of their homes.

The Evil Ones would not give up too easily and would keep trying to break through the enchantment over each of the villages they traveled. Some of the Meronans dared to look out their windows at the dark sky. It seemed the sky was lightening up a bit but there were still a few black capes flying back and forth trying to find an opening or weakness in the enchantment cover.

The Meronans believed in Peace and Harmony which was what their village was known for and how they had all lived for many centuries. Merona was named after a great fairy princess of the same name. She was reputed to have great powers and could see into the future. She had been captured by the Evil Ones a century ago and was never heard from again. Somehow the Meronans felt she still survived and would eventually get back to her home. For the time being Merona was ruled by the Healers.

They had many old and wise Meronans, known to live for more than a century. These men were called Healers who would advise their fellow villagers how to take care of sickness and help in childbirth. The wise Meronans also were able to warn their village of incoming danger.

King Gateskin had received messages from these Healer Meronans and in turn transmitted back to them how to protect their village from the dangers coming their way.

He had warned them beforehand, "The Evil Ones are heading your way, Healers. You must safely tuck your families in the Merona Forest. My men are coming there to help you build a structure to safely contain your families. I am sending a spell to make the structure invisible. Keep your families there until I tell you it is safe."

The Healers had replied, "We will follow your instructions, King Gateskin, in order to keep our village and families safe. Thank you for taking care of us. We are indebted to you."

King Gateskin knew these old Meronans could only do so much to protect themselves and their fellow Meronans with their powers. If the Evil Ones ever broke through the enchanted cover to their village, the Healers of Merona would surely die at the hands of the powerful and evil wizards or they could be captured and brought back to Parotovina and then used against their own people. This, King Gateskin knew, must not be allowed to happen.

VILLAGE OF MERLINA

CHAPTER 15

Merlina shared the largest border with southern
Parotovina. They were located west of Amora,
south of Merona, Sovorotskina and Votovia.
They kept alert at all times and put their own
protective barriers on their border. They could
never be completely safe from the Evil Ones no
matter what they did. They also had to stay ever
vigilant.

Black capes were now seen flying over Merlina by the villagers who rang the alarm in the square which alerted King Zuri and Queen Zuleima in their castle on the hill. The King sent out his men to guard the village and had his powerful wizards and fairies cast protective spells over the land. He had been contacted previously by King Gateskin about the Evil Ones circling the other villages. King Zuri didn't think they were coming his way but he was ready and able to protect his land from them.

King Zuri had his wife, Queen Zuleima, and their children brought to their secret room in the castle which was impervious to any kind of attack. His family was too precious to him. He and his wife were fortunate to have had three children later on in life – two daughters, Zuriann, and Zayleen and a son, Zukan.

The King instructed his family, "You must stay in this room until I say it is safe to come out."

Zukan stepped forward and beseeched, "But, Father, I am old enough to help you with the Evil Ones. Why must I stay here with Mother and my sisters?"

King Zuri looked at his young son. "You must obey me, Zukan. It is for your safety. And, besides I need you to watch over your mother and sisters. They are helpless without you, you know." The King winked at his young son and smiled. They exchanged their special handshakes and pumped fists together.

"Of course, Father. I will do as you say. I will protect my mother and sisters with my life." Zukan bowed to his father and turned back to his mother and sisters who were looking at him with wide, frightened eyes.

"Do not fear, sisters. I am here to protect you." Zukan patted them on their shoulders which he had to stand on tiptoes to do. His mother smiled at her brave son knowing what the exchange was about.

***

The Evil Ones were tiring. They had been traveling back and forth from the villages of Amora, Merona and Votovia. They thought they would at least be able to penetrate one of the villages. Nothing seemed to work out for them.

King Gateskin was keeping in touch with all the villages to ensure they were safe. He opened his mind to the kings and/or healers of each land. Gateskin knew how relentless the Evil Ones could be when they were on a mission.

Gateskin wasn't worried about the village of Merlina. He knew King Zuri was a powerful wizard who could take care of his own village. Even though Merlina did not border Sovorotskina, Gateskin had included Merlina in his promise to the lands bordering his own that he would always watch over them since his land mass was the largest.

King Zuri sent a message to King Gateskin, "Thank you, my friend. I will keep a look out and let you know when the black capes have left. I appreciate your kind support of me and my village."

"You are welcome, King Zuri. I am always here to help. I'm sure the black capes will be leaving soon. They will need to rest. They have traveled all over the land and must be exhausted after their unsuccessful and extensive searches."

"Yes, I agree, King Gateskin. Once they are rested, the Evil Ones will surely try again. I will keep changing my guards so they too can rest until all is quiet and safe in this land."

"That is the right thing to do, King Zuri. I am only a thought away if you need me. Don't hesitate to contact me. I will keep my mind open to you."

"Thank you, Gateskin. I will do that but I think we're safe for now. May you and your village be safe too, my friend."

"Thank you, Zuri. May the gods bless us."

King Zuri looked out over the landscape and saw the black capes moving away. They would be back. King Zuri was sure of it. He had to meet with his guards to formulate the next step if the unmentionable happened.

A STRANGE LITTLE VISITOR

CHAPTER 16

King Gateskin, his family and the Votovian guests were all just sitting down to dinner when they heard a loud booming sound coming from the forest outside their cottage. Then there was a soft knocking at the door, and they all froze. There couldn't possibly be someone out there with the Enchantment Spell protecting them from all sides. It wasn't possible for someone to get through it unless it was one of them.

King Gateskin held up his hand to hold off King Cavelan and all his men as he alone cautiously approached the door. He opened it slowly, peered out and looked down to see a tiny figure standing on the stoop. He had green curly hair and big green eyes and was dressed all in brown looking very much like a tree trunk with legs.

The boy just stood there looking innocently up at the King. He then smiled and bowed to King Gateskin. This boy, just a will-o'-a-wisp, stood about two and a half feet tall.

The boy looked into King Gateskin's eyes and sent him his thoughts, "I am Spindle, one of the Sprites. I live in the surrounding forest of trees around the cottage. I promise I am harmless and a friend of the people of the surrounding villages."

King Gateskin grinned at this little Sprite's words of being harmless. How could he be anything but?

The Sprite continued, "The villagers and Sprites made a pact. They would serve each other in that the villagers would not cut down certain trees where the Sprites lived and the Sprites, in turn, would warn the people of any dangers that may come through the forest."

"Yes, I am aware of our pact with you." The King smiled and waved him on to continue.

Sprindle bowed and said, "Of course, Sorry, King Gateskin."

Spindle added, "There are Evil Ones in the forest trying to break in."

King Gateskin nodded and then inquired, "Are you positive? Did you see them? How many were there? Do you know where they are now?" King Gateskin's face registered alarm as he looked at the young Sprite boy and listened to his thoughts with deep dread and asked his questions.

"Yes, the Evil Ones are trying to get through your enchantment of the trees. I got a little spark from trying to get into one of the trees to get a better view of them. See, I have a burn mark where it zapped me. He held out his right hand to show King Gateskin his burn. Your enchantment is very powerful. We Sprites are not usually affected by such things. We can go through any enchantment without being hurt, well, almost any enchantment, except yours, that is, Your Highness."

"I'm sorry about that, but please go on," the King said with a serious expression of concentration.

"They were too numerous to count," Spindle continued. "They moved back away from the tree line to regroup and try again to break through. They are using a lot of spells and combining their powers; that is the loud booming sound you heard as I got to your door. It made me jump a few feet too. My father said I must warn you of this right away. He fears the Evil Ones will be successful. My father said he owes you a favor for saving my mother when she was pregnant with me many years ago."

"Ah yes, I remember that day," King Gateskin said with a smile.

"I am now 14 years old and the tallest and biggest of all the Sprites," Spindle said this with much pride as he pulled up his chest and threw back his shoulders to make himself look even bigger.

"Father told me to say 'thank you' to Your Highness," the tree Sprite boy bowed at the waist as he said this to King Gateskin and then jumped up in the air to disappear into the trees again before King Gateskin could say 'thank you' back to him.

King Gateskin remembered the day that he had been working in the forest and had been about to cut down a tree when he saw this tiny woman, very pregnant, up in a tree about to fall out of it. He had called up to her to jump and that he would catch her. So, she did jump. He did catch her and put her gently down on the grass. She was a foot tall and light as a feather. She was very tiny in every respect except for the bulge around her middle.

King Gateskin was about to ask her if she was all right when a little man with green hair and a tiny walking stick came out of the forest and bent down to take the woman by the hand and lead her away. He had looked at King Gateskin and nodded his head and sent his thoughts into King Gateskin's head, "Thank you, King

Gateskin for saving my wife and unborn child. I am indebted to you."

The little man's wife had been in labor and had lost her footing in the trees. Sprites are very adept at living in the trees and flying back and forth from tree to tree except when they are pregnant.

As his thoughts came back to the present danger, he closed the door and turned toward the group, sitting anxiously at the table, to explain, "This boy, Spindle, is a sprite. He came to warn us of the Evil Ones close by."

One Votovian replied, "Ah, yes. I have seen these tiny creatures. They are known to be friends to all except the King of Parotovina."

Gateskin responded, "Well, they are good to have as friends since they can see more than we from their vantage point in the trees. I know that the Evil Ones are upset with us for protecting the villages and not allowing them to fulfill their duty to King Kaposkaran."

King Cavelan instructed his men, "I want all of you to station yourselves at each doorway and guard the cottage and extension to protect our women and children in case…"

King Gateskin cleared his throat and said, "Yes, I think that it a good idea, King Cavelan. We have to be on alert." He knew the men needed to feel useful.

The Votovians rose as one and stationed themselves at different places in the large room to guard the cottage and the large addition to protect all the women and children in case the enchantment was broken.

King Gateskin was grateful for their assistance but told them, "We are all safe. The Evil Ones cannot get through the barrier the women had provided to protect us." He knew how strong Queen Solinara's powers were and combined with the powers of all the Votovian women made them even more formidable.

Suddenly it seemed inordinately quiet outside even the Sprites, insects and birds were silent. They all knew something evil was in their midst and were aware that even the slightest noise may bring the evil closer to them.

The children were the only ones who seemed to be having a good time oblivious of what was going on outside the cottage. They were so involved with one another talking or playing with the toys that they did not pay much attention to their parents' anxiety and serious demeanor.

The adults were somewhat relieved to see how unaffected the children were by what was going on around them. The parents wanted to keep their children safe and not cause them needless worry. King Gateskin, along with the other Votovians, had put up the Invisible Soundproof Wall Spell between them and their children which would keep all sounds on their side from reaching the children. At the same time, this barrier would allow the parents to keep a watchful eye and ear on the children. By doing this, the adults could have a meeting and discuss what their next plan of action would be in case the enchantment was broken. The adults were leaning toward sending the children into the trees with the Sprites to hide or just moving the whole cottage and extension to another place under an invisibility cover similar to the one they currently had in effect in the forest.

Unbeknownst to the parents, the children were well aware of what was going on around them having listened in on the conversation between King Gateskin and the Sprite boy before the Soundproof Spell was cast. King Gateskin's children had previously met this Sprite boy, Spindle, when they were out playing in the yard. Spindle had come over to see what the children were playing and wanted to play too. The children and Spindle had become friends in a very short time and shared their thoughts often from a very long distance. At the moment the children were sharing Spindle's thoughts about what their parents would do to protect them.

Spindle reassured the children, "I will keep you abreast of what is happening outside and if we need to run away and hide," the Sprite boy had told them, "I have the very best hiding place and no one would ever find you." Spindle promised to share it with them if they promised not to tell their parents.

The children felt powerful knowing all that was happening without letting their parents become too anxious. They wanted to help in any way they could. After all, they were not babies any more, that is, except for Catalina who was ten.

The children all turned their attention to Catalina who was playing with the other young children stacking blocks and waving her hands back and forth over the blocks. The older children watched in awe as the letters on the blocks spelled out, "**I AM NOT A BABY**!"

CHAPTER 17

Spindle went back to the tree where he lived with his family. His father patted him on the back and said, "Good job, Spindle, I am very proud of you. We must be alert and do what we can to help the Wizard King Gateskin and Fairy Queen Solinara and their friends. It could mean the end of us too if we don't."

Spindle's mother, Anabal, looked at her husband with alarm and shushed him, "Abason, you should not be saying such things in front of our son. You may frighten him. I don't think things are that dire. You know how strong the wizard's powers are and his fairy wife that placed the enchantment along with all the other Votovian women to protect them and us. We will be just fine, dear. Now go along, Spindle, and play with your friends. You do not need to worry about anything, but don't stray too far from the trees. Ok, dear?"

Spindle just shrugged his shoulders and shook his head at his parents who still thought of him as a baby. He flew up into the next tree to look out over the landscape to survey the area. The black capes were nowhere to be seen. They must be hunkering down and discussing their next move. Oh well, he would not worry as his mother had told him and just go find his new friends. His friends were not outside because of the danger nearby but Spindle could send the children his thoughts inside the cottage to see if he could hang out with them again.

"Yes, Spindle, please come in," Serena said as Spindle's thoughts circled around in her head. Spindle was definitely a good friend to have because he could move around without anyone knowing or seeing him due to his diminutive size. Also, Spindle was kind of cute, clever and funny. It was also nice having a friend outside the family who Serena could trust with secrets about her powers.

Serena was anxious to grow up so she could go after the Evil Ones herself and punish them for hurting so many people. She also vowed to her brother, "One day I will go to Parotovina and rescue the families of the Taken Ones from captivity."

"Serena, Mother will never let you go. You are not ready," Simon stressed with a worried frown.

Serena knew her parents would want her to wait a few more years in order to do this at which time her powers would be much stronger. Her mother had promised to help her hone her powers when she was a little older. Each day, though, Serena practiced and practiced all she could to expand and broaden her powers on her own so she would be ready when the time came for her to leave her family and follow her destiny. She sighed as she thought, *my parents think I am still a baby. I am 14 years old now – almost an adult.*

Spindle appeared at the back door and quietly slipped in, blending in with the woodwork, only his green hair being visible. He really enjoyed being with Serena and Simon and all the Votovian children. Spindle especially liked Serena; she was beautiful, very intelligent and her powers were extraordinary. Spindle had a few powers of his own but none that could compare to Serena's. He only wished he were taller because Serena was over five feet tall already.

One look at Serena's beautiful face and Spindle forgot how small he was and ran over to sit next to her on the rug. Spindle gave Serena the most magnificent smile he could and sent his thoughts into her head.

"Oh, that is good to know, Spindle. The black capes are nowhere to be seen. Did you hear that, everyone? You are such a good friend and so helpful to us. We are blind somewhat and you are our eyes and ears. Thank you so much, Spindle, for helping to keep us safe. I hope one day we can repay you for all your kindness."

"I am not being kind, Serena. I want to help. I like you…all of you and I want to help. I have been very lonely and do not have many friends because I am so much bigger than the rest of the Sprites that they feel intimidated by my size. It is funny, isn't it, now I feel intimidated by your size because I am the small one here." Spindle sniggered and looked around at all the smiling faces looking back at him with such kindness in their eyes. Spindle knew he had found a place to be happy and people he could trust and possibly… love.

"You are a big person in our eyes and no different from any of us," Serena said with much conviction. The rest of the children nodded in agreement.

"Thank you for your kindness and for befriending me. I will always do what I can to help you. I always keep my promise too," Spindle's voice choked up as he was trying to hold back tears of happiness at having found so many wonderful friends.

"We know you will, Spindle. We are happy to have you as a dear friend. We will help you and your family in any way we can to keep you all safe too. It is best that we band together for strength. We don't know what to expect in the days to come. One day we will need each other more than ever. I feel there will come a time when we must fight the Evil Ones face to face." Serena shivered at the thought but shook it off. Her eyes and demeanor took on a steely resolve for such a young girl or really a young woman.

"Well, let us put our heads together to come up with a solution to our problems so we can help our parents keep the Evil Ones at bay. Our parents do not know that we are even aware of what is going on around us and we want to keep it that way. We don't want them to worry about us unnecessarily. They do not realize how strong we really are. So, let's play with our toys and act like we don't have a care in the world, for a little while anyway. Ok?"

Serena instructed everyone as she placed the toys around in a circle to demonstrate what her strategy would be. Her parents would not realize what she was doing if they looked over at them. It would look like they were just playing.

CHAPTER 18

Solinara looked over at the children playing with their toys in a circle. They seemed to be so involved in what they were doing. She wondered…what was Serena up to? She could tell by her daughter's face that she was concentrating on something. Solinara tried to read her daughter's thoughts but Serena had put a block on them and all she could read was, Serena was happy with her friends all around her.

Solinara also noticed the Sprite boy, with the green hair, was in the room again. Now, how did he get in without them noticing? Very interesting how the Sprite boy could appear and disappear at will. He could be very helpful to their cause. Solinara made a mental note to speak with Gateskin about this curious little Sprite.

Solinara looked up at her husband who was gesturing with his hands to the Votovian King Cavelan and his guards about the enchantment around their boundaries. Gateskin was a very calming presence to the Votovians who had shown a little anxiety when they had heard the loud boom earlier from the efforts of the Evil Ones trying to enter their protected area.

Gateskin reassured them, "I feel we are well protected and that the enchantment will hold."

Gateskin told the Votovians, "The Evil Ones will get tired and have to go away to rest and regroup. While the Evil Ones are gone, we can reevaluate our options and then discuss it. Then we will just sit tight and wait it out. I do plan on sending messages to all the other villages about doing the same. It is the calm before the next storm."

Gateskin knew the Parotovinans would return but he felt sure he and the Votovians would be ready when the Evil Ones did.

King Gateskin expressed his concerns, "How long would the Parotovinans keep trying before leaving? They would be committing suicide if they went back home without completing their objective. The Evil Ones or EOs knew they could not fail. But could they be persuaded to cross over to the other side and join forces with us? What would that mean to their families who were left behind? Would the EOs' families be in jeopardy?" Gateskin tossed these questions back and forth.

King Gateskin, after much discussion about this with the Votovians, made up his mind to reach the EOs and convince them to join forces with him and that he would help them protect their families from retribution in the event that the EOs did not return to their homeland. King Gateskin would expect, in turn, that the Evil Ones would not harm any of the villagers.

How would King Gateskin convince them of this? How could he protect their families without harm coming to his own? Gateskin had much to work out but he knew he had to come up with a plausible way to make it come to fruition.

After all, King Gateskin was a wizard. He could always use his powers of mind control and persuasion. If that didn't work, he would think of something else.

ONE GOOD MAN

CHAPTER 19

The leader of the scouting party of Parotovinans, Mitteran, gathered his men on the border of the Skina Forest outside the cottage of King Gateskin. Mitteran knew he and his men could not break through the enchantment surrounding King Gateskin's property and all the surrounding villages. Mitteran had underestimated the powers King Gateskin and his friends had. They had skirted all around the borders of Sovorotskina trying to find a way in, to no avail.

Mitteran said to his men, "We have not been successful at any of the villages. That is why I brought you here to this forest where the King of Sovorotskina lives. King Gateskin is a formidable opponent and I fear that we cannot beat him in our usual manner. We must come up with another way to trick him to come to us."

"I will get word to him through the Sprites that I wish to speak with him and make peace. I have never seen a Sprite but I know they are out there listening to us as we speak. I know they will relay my message to King Gateskin. Of course," Mitteran lowered his voice so the Sprites couldn't hear him and continued, "When we meet the King, I will give you the word when to surround and capture him. We will not go home empty handed by any means. It will enable us to keep our lives and those of our families if we do this. There is no other way."

Mitteran looked around at the shocked expressions on the faces of his men. They were not used to doing things this way. The majority of his men were good men, as was he. Mitteran was saying this for the few men who were true Parotovinans who would never go against their King's requests. Mitteran knew some of these men were spies and he had to be ever vigilant in his leadership or they would betray him to King Kaposkaran. A lot of these evil Parotovinans would go to extremes doing evil not only to earn the favor of the King but also because they enjoyed it.

Mitteran was a good man and did not like doing these deeds for the King of Parotovina. But he knew he had to do the King's bidding just to keep his family safe. Mitteran would capture King Gateskin and bring him back to King Kaposkaran. But Mitteran would also try to keep the evil King from harming King Gateskin in any way. He had seen King Gateskin's children playing outside with their father and how much King Gateskin loved them. Mitteran did not want to see the children left fatherless. Mitteran knew how much he loved his own children and how much they would miss him if he did not return to their home.

Though unsavory, the deed must be done but Mitteran would do all he could to keep King

Gateskin safe. He may need King Gateskin's help one day.

A MESSAGE IS DELIVERED

CHAPTER 20

"Spindle, what's wrong? Don't you want to play cards with us anymore?" Serena said to her new friend as she watched him looking out the window of their cottage at the trees.

"Yes, but I have to go. My mother is calling me home. It's important. I will try to return later if

I can." Spindle blended into the wooden door as he passed through it and disappeared outside. In a flash he was up into the trees.

Serena watched Spindle disappeared deep inside the branches of the largest tree. She felt something was not right and could feel a tingling sensation at the back of her neck. Serena had felt this feeling last year just before she was nearly attacked by a wild dog. She had turned in time to look at the dog and controlled his thoughts which prevented the dog from attacking her. Her brother Simon also helped when he flew around the dog's head to distract him. They both got away quickly after the dog became confused and disoriented from Serena's thoughts swirling around in his head. When they relayed this to their father, he captured the dog and brought it further away from their house into the forest of the Unknown Territory. He did not want to kill it but would if it ever came back and threatened his children again.

Serena looked back at her brother Simon, caught his eye and sent her thoughts just to him, "Something is going to happen." Serena had a premonition of danger. Simon nodded at her and went to Serena's side. They exchanged thoughts back and forth showing much wisdom and poise in times of stress in spite of their youth.

"What is it, Serena? What do you see?" Simon asked.

"I don't know but this feeling is not going away," Serena sighed heavily. "I must talk to Spindle."

Serena sent her thoughts to Spindle to try and find out what was going on. She knew from the shivers she was getting up and down her arms that they were all in danger. Serena also felt Spindle knew what this danger was.

When Spindle got back into his tree home, his father took him aside to speak with him in private. This fact made Spindle feel very grown up because he could tell by the look on his father's face that he had something quite serious to share with Spindle and him alone. Spindle did not feel he was in trouble though but that his father needed his help.

"What's wrong, father?" Spindle asked with a worried expression appearing on his little face.

"Well, this is a strange thing, my son. We have been asked or should I say, requested to give a message to King Gateskin from the EOs, the Evin Ones. Some Sprites were at the edge of Skina Forest and overheard the Head Guard, Mitteran, talking to his men. He mentioned that he wanted the Sprites to pass on a message to King Gateskin," Abason shivered involuntarily as he relayed this to his son. He did not want to get involved in any way with the EOs. They could not be trusted.

"What is the message they want us to give to King Gateskin? Is he in danger or are we if we don't give the message to the King?" Spindle furrowed his brow and his face took on an intensely serious look.

Abason thought for a moment then looked at his son with frightened eyes. Spindle's father's eyes never lied and showed all his feelings openly.

This look brought a feeling of dread to Spindle. He had never known his father to be afraid of anyone or anything. Abason was fearless until now. Spindle looked back at his father's distraught face and waited for what would come next, the dreaded message.

CHAPTER 21

"Do you understand what you have to do, Spindle?" Abason looked at his son who towered over him. Spindle was a little large for a tree Sprite who was usually no more than a foot and a half tall, Abason thought. But Abason knew that Spindle's heart and mind were also big and strong. Abason had such aspirations for his son and loved him more than life itself.

Abason and his wife, Anabal, had five children all girls until Spindle. Spindle's sisters were much older than he, all in their twenties. Some of his sisters had families of their own already making Spindle a very young uncle.

Abason had almost given up the idea of ever having a son when Anabal became pregnant late in her forties with Spindle. Sprites can live to be 200 or more. Abason remembered the day when Anabal had fallen out of the tree and was saved by King Gateskin. Abason would have lost both of them if it wasn't for the quick thinking of King Gateskin. Abason owed the King so much. Abason had to help King Gateskin and save him from the Evil Ones.

Abason knew the EOs meant harm to all and would show no mercy. Abason had witnessed their destruction in the past and had narrowly missed being killed when he was the same age as Spindle. If Abason had not been so quick on his feet and had flown up and blended into the highest branches of the trees he would not have survived to talk about it. There were some Sprites that had not been so lucky. Abason's brother, Micah, had been one of them.

Abason felt tears prickle at the back of his eyes at the thought of Micah. Micah had been two years younger and was not as fast as his older brother and had slipped and fallen at the feet of the EOs when they were out in the forest playing. The EOs had taken Micah away and Abason never saw his brother again. Abason only wished he could have saved his brother. That was more than forty years ago. Abason still thought about Micah every day and missed him. His parents had since died without ever knowing what had happened to their youngest son.

Maybe Micah will come back one day...

"Father, are you all right? You seem so far away? I understand what I must do. Are you sure it is safe to do this? What will happen if I bring King Gateskin to them? I really like him and Serena...and Simon and Catalina too, of course. They are my new friends." Spindle felt a warm feeling running through him just thinking of Serena but at the same time was fearful of what could happen to her father and possibly to all of them if he did as he was requested.

"At times we must do something we do not like in order to keep a promise to those we love. I will make sure you and your mother and sisters are all safe. I will also watch over King Gateskin's family until he returns. I don't trust the EOs either, my son. But I do not know what else to do right now."

Spindle noticed his father's usual brown face took on a grey tint as if he were going to be sick.

"Now go on, my son, deliver the message to King Gateskin. The EOs are watching and waiting and they are not patient or forgiving." Spindle nodded to his father and flew out of the tree landing as quietly as a whisper in front of the King's front door. He knocked as loud as his little hand could knock so the King would hear him.

CHAPTER 22

"Well, little man, you are back once again,"
King Gateskin said as he opened the cottage
door. "How do you manage to slip in and out of
my house without me knowing or seeing you?"
King Gateskin smiled as he stood at the door
looking down once again on the little Sprite boy.
He noticed that the boy did not smile as he had
before; in fact, he looked miserable and a little
nervous as he spoke.

"King Gateskin," Spindle said as he bowed to
show respect to this great man and father of his
friend, Serena. "I have come at the request of my

father, Abason. He wanted me to deliver a message to you that he received from the EOs. They request your presence at a meeting in Skina Forest in one hour so they can discuss a peaceful solution to the present circumstances. The EOs asked that you come alone and promised you would not be harmed."

"EOs? Do you mean Evil Ones?"

"Oh yes, my King. We called them EOs."

"Hmm, I see."

King Gateskin noticed the boy's normally brown face looked quite pale and he had a nervous tic at the corner of his right eye. King Gateskin knew this situation was not safe for any of them and that this could lead to his life being taken just to protect his family and friends. King Gateskin felt sorry for the boy since he had to deliver this message under duress. Spindle was definitely not happy about this matter and fear was evident in his eyes.

King Gateskin welcomed the boy into his home and patted him on his head to assure him that it was all right. He told Spindle, "It's okay, little man. Thank you for delivering this message. Go play with the children in the other room but do not mention any of this to them," King Gateskin said. He did not want his children to worry about him unnecessarily.

Spindle nodded solemnly and hurried to the next room where he spotted Serena looking at him with steel in her eyes. He dropped his head and sat down next to her.

In the large dining room King Gateskin announced to King Cavelan and his guards, "There are some new developments."

He whispered to King Cavelin, "We need to cordon ourselves off from the rest of the group by an invisible soundproof wall to ensure privacy."

Gateskin did this quickly and continued with his news, "I did not want anyone to be frightened about their safety. The Sprite boy, Spindle, came to give me this message from his father. The EOs, Evil Ones, request a meeting in the forest with me and me alone. This has now changed what I had planned to do, King Cavelan."

"I see. Do you think it is safe for you to go alone, Gateskin?" King Cavelan asked warily.

"They specifically requested I go alone. I have no choice in the matter, Cavelan. I must do this. I had planned to meet the leader of the scouting party anyway. This is my chance to convince him to switch sides. But it may just work out for me in the long run."

"I can send my guards with you," King Cavelan insisted.

"No, I will go alone as requested. I do not want to endanger their lives too." He knew he may not return from this meeting and did not want to take anyone with him.

King Cavelan's guards stood firm in solidarity to protect King Gateskin.

Gateskin finally convinced the guards, "You must stay at the cottage and extension in order to protect the rest of the group."

Gateskin promised, "I will return as soon as possible but if I do not return, you are to continue to protect and defend the families and the village."

Gateskin went to see Solinara to say goodbye and to kiss and hug his children before he left. It may be the last time he would see any of them.

The hair was standing up on Gateskin's arms and the back of his neck. This was not a good sign of what was to come.

Solinara held onto Gateskin, not wanting to let go. Gateskin explained to her, "It is just a meeting, dear. I will return very soon. You should not worry for it may cause the children to be unnecessarily concerned."

"You must be vigilant, Gateskin. I'm worried. Please come back to us," Solinara sighed and felt a shiver going through her at the thought of her husband being in danger.

Gateskin also told the children, "Listen, dear ones, I have a meeting and will return shortly. Please take care of your mother until I return."

The children looked up at their father with love and trust in their eyes. But somehow King

Gateskin could see much wisdom in Serena's eyes as she smiled, nodded and hugged him tightly before turning to go back to her friends. Simon had given him a quick hug and shook his hand firmly, for he was growing up to be a big boy now. Catalina still a little girl kissed him all over his face causing him to laugh out loud at her antics.

As King Gateskin turned away from his family, his life, his loves, he felt as if he were being pulled away from every thing he held most dear to him. Gateskin had to be strong and survive whatever he had to face so he could return to his family and keep them safe at all costs.

Gateskin looked at his wife and smiled and felt her love and strength flowing through him. Her thoughts were in his head and he nodded to his Queen, "I will be careful and alert."

He sent his thoughts back to her, "You should not worry about me. I will do all I can to return safely to you and our children."

Gateskin opened the door and walked out as Solinara stood at the door and spread her fingers towards the trees to provide an opening in the enchanted barrier so Gateskin could go into the forest for his meeting with the EOs. The area turned red as the barrier opened and Gateskin passed through, then immediately it closed behind him changing back to the trees.

The air suddenly seemed like it had left his chest as Gateskin passed through the barrier. He turned to gaze at his wife who was still standing at the door looking at him. Gateskin raised his hand through the tree barrier to Solinara making a sign that everything was going to be all right. She smiled back at him and made her own sign back that she would be watching over him.

Gateskin looked around him but all was peaceful and deathly quiet. He couldn't even hear the birds or insects. It was as if they were hiding away sensing the danger afoot. Gateskin wondered why he was there, but then his thoughts went to his family and the others…he knew he had no other choice.

CHAPTER 23

"Spindle, you are back. What happened? You look kind of pale. Are you all right?" Serena looked at Spindle's face and noted his usually happy demeanor was gone and in place of it an aura of anxiety surrounded him.

Spindle looked up at Serena with glazed and vacant eyes no longer green but deep dark brown mirroring his emotions. Spindle couldn't speak because he was afraid to tell her anything that would make her upset. But at the same time, he knew very shortly Serena would know the terrible truth; her father was in danger.

"You know I can concentrate and decipher your thoughts eventually so you might as well tell me what is going on," Serena said this with such a strong voice that it was more of a command than a request.

"Well, I didn't want to give him the message but my father insisted that it was the right thing to do. I fear for his safety and I know my father does too. My father did promise to watch over your father as closely as he can and will get word to your mother if your father needs any assistance," he rambled on, not really explaining to Serena.

"Now Spindle, please start at the beginning. You are telling the ending before the beginning. Are you talking about my father being in danger of someone or something? Where is he? My father was just in to see us and he said he had a meeting and... Where did he go, Spindle? Tell me quickly, where did my father go?" Serena's voice became shaky and her eyes were wide and frightened. She grabbed Spindle by the arm as she looked at him waiting to hear more.

"I am so sorry, Serena. I wanted to tell you but my father thought it best to keep quiet. Your father told me to come here and spend time with you and the other children and not to worry."

Spindle took a deep breath before he continued, "My father was given a message from the EOs to relay to your father. They said they wanted to meet with King Gateskin to discuss the present situation between them. What could I do? I had to deliver the message." Spindle sighed heavily and said, "What can I do to help? I can go and spy on him for you to make sure he is all right." Spindle's sad face showed how contrite he was.

"It's okay, Spindle. I am not blaming you. I know you were just doing as your father requested. I am truly worried about my father. The EOs, Evil ones, I think you mean, cannot be trusted. They would surely harm him. I couldn't bear to lose him!" Serena choked up as the prospect of anything happening to her father became too surreal.

Simon, sensing his sister's distress, rushed to her side. She sent her thoughts to Simon and to Catalina, "We must prepare ourselves in case our father needs our help. It seems the time has finally come for us to fulfill our destiny and confront the Parotovinans."

Serena was concerned about her younger siblings and by the fact that their involvement in this adventure could endanger their lives. But she knew that they would not let her go alone. They would come after her. She would do what she could to keep them safe even if it took her own life to do it.

Serena could feel her father close by. His thoughts flooded into her head. He was wandering around the forest outside the enchanted boundaries of their home. She could also feel the danger encroaching around him. She let out a muffled cry. Simon and Catalina looked at her and read her thoughts. They were not as close to their father's thoughts as Serena was.

Serena looked at Simon and Catalina and sent them calming thoughts to allay their fears that all was going to be okay. They smiled wanly at her but their furrowed brows did not deceive her from seeing that they were also anxious about their father's safety.

Serena spoke quickly with Spindle, "Can you come with us, Spindle?"

"Of course, Serena. I will be by your side whenever and wherever you need me to be." Spindle bowed to Serena in reverence.

Serena patted Spindle on the head and said, "Please, Spindle. It is not necessary for you to bow to me."

"Oh yes, my lady. You are a princess after all. Your father is the King of Sovorotskina."

The other children watched this display and bowed in turn to Serena. Serena just shook her head and gave up. She waved at everyone to please stand up.

Some of the other older children wanted to go with them but she convinced them, "You must stay to help out the adults. Every hand will be needed to keep the EOs at bay." Serena was also worried about her mother and how upset she would be when she learned that they had gone after their father.

Serena decided she would have to talk to her mother about what her intentions were and convince her that it was the only solution to the problem. The Evil Ones would not expect children to be of any trouble to them. They did not know the powers King Gateskin's offspring had and if combined how unbeatable they could be.

Serena sent her thoughts to Simon and Catalina that she was going to see their mother and tell her of their plans. They had looked up at her with reservation and consternation visible on their faces.

Simon and Catalina asked Serena through their thoughts, "Do you want us to go with you to see Mother?"

Serena shook her head at them and smiled. "No, I think I need to speak with Mother alone."
They could see from Serena's thoughts that she just may convince their mother it was the right thing to do.

A TOUGH DECISION IS MADE

CHAPTER 24

Queen Solinara sat at the table in her husband's seat as she discussed with the Votovians where King Gateskin was going and with whom he was meeting. Their faces registered deep concern and some consternation over King Gateskin's decision to do this on his own.

The Votovian guards told Queen Solinara, "Dear Queen, we wanted to go with King

Gateskin but he had insisted on going alone. He told us that we were needed here to ensure the safety of our families and the village."

The guards promised Queen Solinara, "We will do whatever we can to get King Gateskin back safely and also to keep all of us safe at your home."

"Thank you all for your help. I know you will do everything in your power to keep us safe, as will I."

Queen Solinara had gotten up from the table after the discussion with the Votovian King and his guards and felt a little more hopeful that things would work out for King Gateskin. She kept her thoughts with her husband and sent her protective powers to give him strength. But Queen Solinara suddenly felt her protective power waning and growing thinner as he got further away from her as he traveled deeper into the forest.

Solinara was so intensely focusing her thoughts on her husband that she did not see her daughter, Serena, standing in front of her until she felt Serena's hand on her arm. Solinara felt a sudden jolt at the same time from her husband that he had been surrounded by the Evil Ones and was in grave danger.

Solinara looked down at her daughter as tears formed in her eyes. Serena was at once alarmed at her mother's face which had gotten so pale and her eyes were brimming with tears.

"Mother, what is wrong?" Serena asked with alarm. But before her mother could answer Serena saw through her father's thoughts, as they began to jump into her head in a jumbled mass, that he was being surrounded by men in black capes – the Evil Ones!

"Oh no, mother, they tricked him! They did not mean to talk with him. We should have known he would be in danger. I sensed something was wrong and that is why I came to see you. I need to talk to you about Father. I...I mean...we want to go after them to get Father back. We now know where they are taking him and why. They will use him against us. You know Father will not help them destroy the enchantment around the villages so that they can have Taken Ones or the TOs to bring back to their king. We have to do something and we cannot wait much longer.

The EOs or Evil Ones will surely kill him!" Serena felt her own tears burning her eyes as she spoke the words that hurt her more than she could say.

"Serena, I do not want to worry about you, your brother and sister too. Your father will use his powers to get himself out of this situation. I cannot lose you three also! I just could not go on! Your father will keep sending his thoughts to me and I will send all my powers to help him. He will not be alone. You must not do this thing! You will not survive. I have not yet helped you hone your powers. It is too soon for all of you to do this on your own. You will need help." Solinara put her head into her hands as the tears ran through her fingers.

"Mother, please don't cry and worry about us. We will be safe. We will keep our thoughts with yours at all times. We will combine our powers and will be treble strong. I have been working on my powers and have learned a lot and have helped Simon and Catalina with their powers. We did not want you to worry about us so we have been preparing for this day over the past few years. We may be young but we are strong and smart like you and father. You have taught us well by example." Serena put her arms around her mother and held her tightly.

Solinara hugged her eldest child fiercely to her chest and kissed her on her forehead. She then held her at arms length to study Serena and noticed how much she had grown. Solinara noted also, Serena would probably be taller than she within a few years. Her daughter's eyes mirrored a strength and resilience well beyond her years.

Solinara smiled at her beautiful daughter then announced to her, "Serena, I give you my permission to go on this adventure but you must promise me to keep your brother and sister safe. There is one other condition, too, that you travel with the aid of a fairy and wizard, your Aunt Procelina and Uncle Hotenfaran. I will get word to them to meet you on the road outside the village. Then and only then will I feel better about you venturing out."

Serena nodded in agreement. She had met Aunt Procelina and Uncle Hotenfaran, her mother's brother and sister-in-law when she was just a toddler. They had both been very funny and quite the characters, if she remembered correctly. They had sent the three children presents on their birthdays each year and on the village holidays too. One of her aunt's and uncle's presents to her was a book of chants and spells which Serena has been studying for the past several years with which to hone her powers. It had been most helpful. She had hoped to use some of these spells to rescue their father.

Solinara read Serena's thoughts and said, "My child, please be very careful with those spells and chants that your aunt and uncle gave you in the book. They have not always worked for them in the past. They can be tricky and need to be practiced carefully and not on each other but on inanimate objects that cannot be harmed. Be careful also of others who can read your thoughts. Use the Block Enchantment to keep your thoughts to yourself at all times and allow only your siblings to hear them. You will find that one on page 141. I put that one in there for my brother."

"I understand, Mother. I will be careful," Serena nodded.

"We put our spells in there when we were just children. Then Hotenfaran changed them a little and made them stronger and more effective as he got older. Please check with him before using some of them to make sure they are up to date. He has a habit of changing things the last minute or leaving a crucial thing out of the spells. I love my brother but he can be a little eccentric at times."

Solinara tittered as thoughts of her brother mixing the chants and spells when they were children and nearly blowing up their house came into her head. They did have some fun times together and these thoughts made her realize how much she missed Hotenfaran. He was a gypsy of sorts as was his wife, Procelina. They never stayed in one place for very long. She knew she could trust him though to take care of her children. The children would be safe with him and Procelina. Solinara planned to keep her thoughts open to her brother and sister-in-law so they could keep in touch with her and keep her aware of what they were doing and where they were at all times.

Solinara thought, she must not lose her husband and her children to the EOs…she could not and would not allow it! She felt her resolve growing stronger once again and she opened her thoughts to her husband. Gateskin's thoughts were faint as if he were being held in a place that contained Staglemite. This was a substance that acted like a filter that could trap thoughts in it and prevent thoughts from coming or going. They must know this is one way to control him. There is a way to get through it...I must think. Hortenfaran discovered this Staglemite by accident when we were children. He knows how to get around it. I must talk to him right away.

Solinara turned to her daughter and told her, "Get ready, sweetheart, for your long journey. I will be there to help you all shortly. There are some things I need to attend to first."

"Thank you, Mother. We will do that right away."

Solinara sent her thoughts to her brother. He did not answer right away. He must be distracted as usual, she thought. She sent her thoughts to Procelina also and received word right away. Solinara told Procelina of the children's plans and her difficulty reaching Gateskin's thoughts.

"I will relay your message, Queen Solinara, and have him get back to you right away. You know how your brother can be. He gets busy and doesn't always listen to messages that come his way." Procelina also said, "Please do not worry. Your children will be safe with us. I guarantee that we will act as parents toward them and keep them out of danger even if it takes our lives."

Solinara felt relief flooding through her as Procelina relayed these messages. "Thank you, dear Procelina. I knew I could always count on you both in times like these."

Serena knew that her brother and sister-in-law may not have kept in close proximity to her and her family over the years but they could always be trusted to help whenever they were needed.

THE ADVENTURE BEGINS

CHAPTER 25

Solinara rounded up some of her Memory Stones that would help her children remember all the spells and chants just by holding the stones in their hands until they felt warm to the touch. She explained this to them and packed several small stones in each of their packs.

Solinara also put in a scroll with a message to give to their father once they found him, in case she could not send messages to him through her thoughts. The scroll was blank but once he took it in his hands it would print out for his eyes only to see. She wrote what she could not say out loud and then she signed it, 'Your Loving Wife, Solinara.'

But the Queen knew King Gateskin would do all he could to save their children from the evil fate of the King of Parotovina even if he had to die to accomplish this. Solinara hoped and prayed it would not come to that. She couldn't imagine living without her husband.

Solinara packed the children some water, dried fruit, cured and salted meat, and bread and cheese she had made that morning, enough to last them for a week. Solinara knew the children would be able to provide for themselves after that with the aid of their powers and those of Hotenfaran and Procelina.

Solinara hugged each of her children and then cast a spell over them as they turned and walked away from her to keep them safe from any harm. Solinara knew the spell would last for a little while anyway. Once the children reached the border of Merona where they would meet their aunt and uncle, Hortenfaran would redo the spell to ensure it lasted throughout the rest of the trip.

Solinara stood at the door and waved goodbye to them as she opened the enchanted boundary to allow them to pass through. As she was doing this, she noticed the little brown, Sprite, Spindle, when he jumped out of the large tree near the boundary and joined her children on their adventure. He had a pack on his back that was bigger than he. Spindle was struggling under the weight of it. Queen Solinara waved her hand over Spindle's pack and lightened it so he could carry it more easily.

Spindle at once noticed his load was a lot lighter and turned to wave at Queen Solinara to say 'thank you.' Spindle had seen Queen Solinara standing at the door watching Serena, Simon, and Catalina with such a profound look of sadness on her face. He knew Queen Solinara was a kind woman and very powerful, not only in her abilities, but also in her character.

Spindle gave Queen Solinara his most radiant smile to let her know, "I will watch over your children to the best of my ability as a little person."

Queen Solinara sent her thoughts back to Spindle, "I appreciate that you will be with my children and know that you will do all you can to help them succeed on this dangerous journey." Queen Solinara continued, "I promise to bake you a special gooseberry pie if you bring them all back unharmed."

Spindle's smile only got wider at the prospect of one of Queen Solinara's pies. "Thank you, my Queen!" Spindle bowed to Solinara.

Spindle remembered back when he had stolen a bite out of one of Queen Solinara's pies after he had spied it on the windowsill one morning several years ago. He blushed at the thought of it and realized Queen Solinara had known that he was the culprit. Queen Solinara smiled back at Spindle to let him know all was forgiven. Spindle skipped on his way to catch up to the children and waved at Queen Solinara as he passed through the boundary.

Solinara raised her hand at all of them one last time before the boundary closed and then she turned away to face the challenge of being the only member of her family left in the cottage to protect and defend the Votovians and the villagers.

She only prayed that she would be able to do her duty as Queen and keep everyone safe in her village while she kept her thoughts on her husband and children's safe return home.

CHAPTER 26

Queen Solinara looked at King Cavelan and Queen Savina who were standing next to the table exchanging worried looks. Savina quickly came forward and hugged Solinara, smoothing her hair down, as she patted her on the back to try to comfort her. Queen Savina couldn't imagine her children doing something like this and if she would have been as strong as Queen Solinara.

Solinara stepped back from the embrace and smiled at Queen Savina in gratitude. She said, "Queen Savina, you are most kind. It is good to have a friend close by in times like this. It is going to be a tough time not only for me but for all of us, if King Gateskin does not return. I do not like to even think about this possibility. I know King Gateskin will do all he can to get away. He knows the children are coming, I am sure. I did send this message to his mind before it was closed off by the Staglemite. Gateskin was upset about it but he knew how stubborn Serena could be once she made up her mind to do something. She is a lot like her father and Gateskin knows that."

King Cavelan stepped forward to offer his help. He promised, "I will send two of my guards out to the forest and beyond to ensure that there are no Evil Ones left out there. The guards will also scout around the area for any evidence of a struggle on the part of King Gateskin that could give them some help in finding him. King Gateskin may have left some clue as to what they were planning to do with him."

Queen Solinara thanked King Cavelan, "I appreciate your assistance and kindness, King Cavelan. I still fear what the EOs can do."

"EOs? Are we to call them that instead of Evil Ones?" King Cavelan asked.

"Yes, Serena told me that is what everyone calls them."

"Then we will call them that too. Is there anything else I can help you with, Queen Solinara."

"No, thank you, King Cavelan. I need to think and pray now."

King Cavelan bowed to the Queen and stepped aside to let her pass.

The Queen turned and went into her bedroom to think in solitude about what she would do if anything should happen to her family. Queen Solinara knelt in front of the statues of the god and goddess of light and goodness Ressaphena and Ramoforan. She fervently prayed for their intervention on behalf of her family to bring them back to her safely. She also prayed she would have the strength and courage to go on if…she couldn't bring herself to even think such things out loud.

Solinara would remain confident and positive that they would return unharmed together. She would continue to send positive thoughts to her husband and children not only for them but to bolster her own confidence and spirits until they could return to her. In the meantime, Queen Solinara needed to keep herself busy and mentally prepared for whatever would happen, so she left her room and returned to the table where the Votovians were still discussing their next moves.

As Queen Solinara entered the room, their conversations quieted down and they all turned to look at her. Queen Solinara smiled the most confident smile purely from her heart that she could muster without using her fairy powers. Queen Solinara's beautiful smile was met with many pure smiles from all those at the table. The Votovians rose to acknowledge Queen Solinara and requested her presence at the table once again to continue their latest discussion.

King Cavelan told Queen Solinara, "My guards found a piece of King Gateskin's leather vest that had gotten stuck on a branch a short distance off the path where he was dragged. There were marks of a scuffle and many feet around the area where King Gateskin was lifted and carried away. King Gateskin had time enough to draw a circle in the dirt under him with a line crossing at its center before he was taken."

Queen Solinara thought about the circle with the line down the center. She knew he was trying to tell them something. What could it be? She wondered.

Queen Solinara pulled out the map of Sovorotskina and the surrounding villages and placed it in the middle of the table. King Cavelan leaned over to look at it more closely. As they were all studying the map a circle with a line down the middle appeared in the southern part of the mountains near Parotovina. King Gateskin had somehow managed to send this last message to them. They now knew where he was being kept prisoner by the EOs...at the base of Crotesia Mountain.

Queen Solinara stated, "It looks as if they are not bringing him back to their village right away. They may be trying to get information out of him beforehand to ensure that they had something to bargain with when they met with King Kaposkaran."

Queen Solinara concentrated and sent her thoughts to her brother and sister-in-law of this new development. She told them, "You do not need to enter Parotovina just yet. You must travel to the base of the southern mountain of Crotesia on the border of Amora and Parotovina. That is where the EOs are keeping Gateskin. There is a large cave there that is used to store many of the Parotovinan peoples' supplies and weapons. It was long known as a meeting place for the EOs, a place for them to gather and strategize prior to their travels to the villages to obtain more Taken Ones."

Solinara at once heard her brother's thoughts come back to her, "Dear Solinara, we will indeed find this cave and try to surprise the Evil Ones or EOs and convince them to release King Gateskin to us." Hotenfaran further assured Queen Solinara, "I will do it carefully using my persuasive powers. You need not worry about the children. I will make sure they are all safe and have a wonderful time on this adventure."

"Thank you, dear brother, for your kindness in doing this for me. I know it is a lot to ask and that you will do all you can to keep my children safe and bring Gateskin and them back to me. Please be careful. I miss you, big brother. I will keep sending my thoughts and powers to you to help you along the way. Give my children my love when you meet them. Tell them to listen to you and follow your instructions at all times. I know Serena can be trying at times. But she is a good girl. Simon is a little man now and he will do all he can to make you proud of him. As for Catalina, she is a little princess, sweet and loving and trusting of everyone. Simon is more of a skeptic but he will watch over his baby sister to make sure she makes the right decisions and is safe. I look forward to seeing you all back in Sovorotskina soon, I hope. Take care, Hotenfaran. I love you."

Hotenfaran felt his eyes burning with unspent tears at what his sister had said. "I promise, Solinara, to do all I can. I love you too, sister!" He smiled and sniffed as he and Procelina continued on their way to meet the children. Now they had a plan and a definitive place to go.

Procelina looked at her husband and noticed his eyes glistened where tears threatened to fall. She asked, "Is everything okay, my love?"

"Yes, dear, all is right and proper. We are heading to Crotesia Mountain where Gateskin is being held in the cave."

Procelina nodded and smiled for she had already heard the whole conversation after she had tapped into her husband's mind.

A FAMILY REUNION

CHAPTER 27

Serena walked along the path and kept looking back at Simon and Catalina to ensure they were still there. That's when she noticed Spindle hopping along behind them. She thought that he wasn't going to come with them. Serena felt a funny flushing feeling of her cheeks when she realized that she was relieved to see his smiling face looking back at her.

Spindle ran ahead and walked alongside Serena, which was hard to do, since she was taking bigger steps than his short legs could take to keep up with her. Serena looked down at Spindle and noticed he was huffing and puffing alongside her. She slowed her pace a little and Spindle smiled up at her and nodded, sending his gratitude into her thoughts. Serena found herself smiling back at Spindle and taking his hand in hers, moved together as one.

Simon and Catalina were walking hand in hand too and raced forward to get in step with them. Simon was always very protective of his little sister and had promised his mother he would take care of Catalina.

They looked like a small party of happy children, who did not have a care, to the outside world. They wanted to look innocent and powerless to anyone who may pass by. The children did not want to give the EOs any inclination of what they had planned to do.

There were more people on the roads now since the EOs had left. Serena kept her mind open to the thoughts of those who passed by and could hear only that the children were thought of as sweet innocents who were out for a stroll or picnic since they carried baskets and packs with food. Some of these people did show some concern, however, for the safety of the children walking without any adults.

Serena sent some calming thoughts back to them that they were indeed out for a stroll and a picnic with friends and were safe from harm. Serena had safely blocked out all of their real plans from anyone to read.

As the children came closer to Gateskin River, they had to find a spot that was low enough to cross or use their powers to fly over it with Simon's help. Simon spoke up when he heard his sister's thoughts.

"I will handle this, Serena. Take my hand and I will fly you over the river. You too, Catalina. Come here." With both of his sisters' hands in his, he flew them over the river which was much too high to traverse by foot.

"Thank you, Simon. I hadn't thought about the river when we started off. Actually, I forgot all about it. It is too deep for us to go by foot. I'm sorry about that. It wasn't good planning on my part. I am supposed to be on top of things to keep you both safe. I promised Mother I would."

"Don't worry, Serena. That is why we are a team. We help each other, remember?" Simon gave his sister a high five to calm her down.

"I guess you're right, Simon. Of course, I will need your help along the way. Thank you."

"What about me, Serena? I am part of this team. You will need my help too," Catalina piped in.

"Yes, of course, my little sister. I always need your help. You have much power that will be needed on our journey."

Catalina smiled broadly and hugged Serena in thanks. "Yes, you will, big sister. You certainly will," Catalina giggled.

The children had now reached the border of Merona and saw up ahead two tall figures coming toward them very fast. Serena put her hands up to feel the vibrations in the air and to try to read the thoughts of these two figures to find out what their intentions were. Before

Serena could come up with anything definitive, the tall figures stood in front of her smiling and bowing and the next minute Serena was being swung around by Uncle Hotenfaran and then kissed and hugged by Aunt Procelina.

Catalina clapped her hands and said, "Me next?" While Simon tried to find something to hide behind, the last thing he wanted was to be picked up like a baby and hugged and kissed.

Aunt Procelina picked up Catalina and proceeded to ooh and aah over how big she had gotten. Procelina was well aware of Simon trying to hide from her. So Procelina walked right past him and looked down at Spindle and said, "Now, who do we have here? I don't remember ever meeting this little man. What is your name, my fine green-headed boy?" Procelina gave him her sweetest smile so as not to frighten him away. She was a sight to see.

Spindle introduced himself and said, "I am happy to meet you both and have heard good things from Serena about you." He told Procelina, "The Book of Spells that you gave Serena was really 'green.'" 'Green' was the

Sprites word for 'cool!' Spindle looked with awe at Procelina as she shook his hand.

Procelina bowed to Spindle and her eyes sparkled as she looked down at him.

This powerful fairy had long, wild, wiry dark brown hair sprinkled with gray and white that stood up on its own accord going in every direction imaginable. She wore a long caftan of brilliant colors that swept the ground and flowed around her as she walked. The most remarkable things about her, though, were her eyes – a cerulean blue, bright and cheery with an intelligent and kind gleam to them.

Hotenfaran, on the other hand, had a long white beard and his white hair was also long and fell down beyond his shoulders. He wore a tall hat that had tassels in different colors hanging from its point. Hotenfaran also wore a long caftan but his was in muted shades of green and gold that seemed to shimmer in the light of day. His eyes were very dark brown but had speckles of gold in them that sparkled when he was happy as he was now.

Once all the commotion had died down, Simon finally came forward from his hiding place and extended his hand to his uncle and aunt to show them he was now a man. Simon told them of the purpose of their journey. "We are going to find our father and free him from the EOs."

Hotenfaran nodded and shook Simon's hand and smiled at his nephew who seemed to favor his father in looks and temperament. "Yes, we are here to assist you on your journey. You said, EOs meaning Evil Ones?"

"Yes, it was how most of us identify them. Spindle told us that is what the Sprites call them."

"Oh, I see," Hotenfaran said with a smile at Simon who was acting all grown up.

Procelina took Simon's hand in hers and pressed it tightly looking into his eyes and hearing his thoughts. Procelina could tell Simon was excited about this adventure but at the same time he was apprehensive about its outcome. Simon feared for his father's life more than his own. "Please do not worry. We will do this together and keep you all safe."

Of course, Hotenfaran and Procelina had long ago sent their thoughts to Queen Solinara to reassure her all would be well with the children. The fairy and wizard had been watching the children from a long distance away to ensure that they were safe from anyone or anything as they traveled from their cottage in Merona through the woods to the border of Sovorotskina.

The wizard and fairy had admired the ingenuity of the children to cross the river by flying over it. They had wondered if they would have to come to their rescue. The river was quite deep and rough to traverse.

"We were quite impressed at your expertise in traversing the river. That was something to see!" Procelina said as she had laughed at the sight of the three children flying over the river.

Simon explained with pride, "It was me doing that. I can fly and do other things too."

"Well, you certainly did a wonderful job of flying you and your sisters over the rising river."

Simon swelled even more at the compliment from his powerful aunt.

Procelina was a powerful fairy with great powers of sight and hearing. Not only were her eyes beautiful but they could see miles away and pictures came into her mind as she looked through the forest and at the travelers around them. She could hear a pin drop in a pile of hay. She was always alert and on guard.

Hotenfaran had his own magical powers. He could fly around and become invisible, blending in with his surroundings. This came in handy when he wanted to spy on anyone. He could also make objects or people disappear. All he had to do was wave his hands over anything and it would disappear and then reappear somewhere else.

They were definitely the perfect pair to aid the children on their journey. This is why Queen Solinara had chosen them. Solinara knew her brother and his wife loved her children. They would make sure the children were safe at all times. After all, Hotenfaran and Procelina were family.

Hotenfaran and Procelina were never able to have any children of their own and Queen Solinara knew how much they had wanted them when they were younger. This would be a good bonding experience for her brother and his wife to be with her children. Hotenfaran and Procelina may change their minds about wanting children after this adventure was over.

Solinara had explained all about her children to her brother and his wife so they would know what to expect. After all, they had not seen them since they were quite young.

"There are some things you must know about my children. My son, Simon can be quite trying. He is stubborn like his father. Serena is determined when she wants to do something on her own." Solinara only hoped Serena did not cause her aunt and uncle too much difficulty. Solinara would have thought this was humorous if she hadn't been so distraught about their safe return home.

"Now Catalina is no problem at all, she is always so sweet and loving and only wants to please everyone. I worry about her safety because of this. I know Simon will watch over her, for he loves Catalina as much as I do. Catalina, though only ten, is a very strong-willed little girl and is blessed with great powers for such a young person. She can take care of herself to some extent as long as she doesn't trust every person she meets. Catalina has a tendency to love everyone and never thinks ill of anyone either."

Solinara had explained further, "While Catalina is trusting, Simon is skeptical of everything and everyone. They balance each other out."

Hotenfaran and Procelina had assured Solinara, "Please do not worry about them. We are here to ensure they are taken care of and will not leave them out of our sight."

Solinara sighed in relief and had said, "Thank you. I won't worry too much. But you know me I can't help myself. Thank you. I love you both."

***

Serena was relieved to be with her aunt and uncle. She had so much to ask them about the Book of Spells that they had given her. Serena had been studying it ever since she was just a toddler and had learned to read at an early age. Serena's parents had seen her looking at the book on many occasions, but they were not yet aware of Serena's reading abilities. Her parents had thought Serena was just looking at the drawings and pictures.

At first Serena did not understand some of the spells, but as she grew older, the spells made more sense to her as her powers became stronger. Serena had almost perfected the Disappearing Spell, one that her uncle could do without thinking. Serena would have to him about one part of it she kept getting stuck on, leaving Serena only half invisible.

CHAPTER 28

The party of six walked three by two down the dusty road heading toward their destination – the Cave in the southernmost mountain of Crotesia. Hotenfaran walked in the lead with Serena while Spindle skipped along next to them trying to keep up with their fast pace. Following behind them were Procelina and Simon and holding tightly to her brother's hand, was Catalina.

They had to pass through the village of Merona and then into Amora before arriving at Mt. Crotesia. They had many miles to traverse yet. Hotenfaran had been speeding up their travel without any one of the children knowing. He knew they didn't have much time to waste. He feared for the safety of his brother-in-law. Once he made a promise, he always kept it. This promise was the most important one he ever had made – to keep his sister's children safe and find her husband and return all of them safely home.

The village was peaceful and absent of any traffic since the EOs had tried to break the barriers. The villagers were still holding up in their cottages for safety until there was an all clear from Gateskin which wouldn't come until he was freed. Each cottage they passed the group noticed some heads at the windows watching them. Most likely they were curious why this group of children and adults were passing through their village.

The group was talking in close whispers as they moved along the road. Procelina was totally aware of their surroundings and kept scanning the woods in front, behind and on both sides of them. She did not sense any problems or dangers to them but sent her thoughts to Hotenfaran who looked back at her and nodded when he saw a wagon up ahead on the side of the road.

As they got closer, they noticed a man on the ground trying to fix the spoke of a wheel that had split after hitting a rock. Hotenfaran raised his right hand to alert his party to stop.

He sent his thoughts to Procelina, "Stay here while I find out who this man is and where he is going."

She nodded and told him, "I will keep them back until you send word to do otherwise, dear."

The children were getting restless after several minutes had gone by and still no word from Hotenfaran about whether they could continue on or not. Procelina reassured them all was well and if there was any danger, he would have alerted her right away. Anyway, with her extensive powers, she would have felt it long before he sent word to her.

Procelina watched and listened to the exchange between her husband and the man on the road ahead. It seemed that the man had been run off the road by the EOs who were in a hurry a couple of hours back. The man had been trying to fix his wheel ever since and was about to give up when Hotenfaran came along to offer his assistance.

They talked extensively about what the man had seen and how many EOs had passed by. Hotenfaran also asked, "Did you notice the EOs carrying a large bundle of sorts?"

The man replied, "Yes, I did notice there was a large bundle they had strapped to their horse drawn cart and that it kept making noises and jumping around. I was curious about what could be in the bundle but did not dare ask for they would have strung me up just for asking." The man added, "I heard the EOs talking amongst themselves about heading to the cave of the mountain called Crotesia."

After Hotenfaran had gotten all the information he could out of the man, he offered to fix the man's wagon wheel so he could be on his way. The man was surprised when Hotenfaran got down on the ground and laid his hands over the wheel and pressed tightly on the spoke that had broken. Before the man's very eyes the spoke fixed itself and straightened out. Hotenfaran lifted the wagon back onto the road and the man hopped up onto the front seat, took the reins of his horses and off he went. He tipped his hat and bowed his thanks to Hotenfaran as he rode away. He could be heard yelling back, "I owe you much, my friend. I will repay you one day."

Hotenfaran lifted his hat and waved at the man and bowed back to him saying, "Take care, my friend, and may you have a safe journey home."

Procelina gathered the children together and moved forward as she was instructed by her husband, all was now clear. The man was not a danger but, on the contrary, had been a great help to them. He confirmed the fact that the EOs had indeed kidnapped King Gateskin and that they were taking him to the Cave as they had suspected.

Hotenfaran was expecting the Cave to be well guarded and he sent his thoughts to Procelina so she could scan and listen to the countryside to see if she could pick up any large parties moving about. Hotenfaran wanted to ensure the safety of his nieces and nephew and their Sprite friend.

As they moved further through the village, they notice more people. Since the black capes had left, some people were beginning to move about again but still wary of where they were going or how far. Their leaders had told them to be watchful until they heard from King Gateskin. The group greeted the people with nods and waves as they passed through.

The travelers still had a day's journey ahead to the cave and planned to stop within the next few hours to take a rest and get some nourishment before continuing on until dark. Hotenfaran knew that they could not fly to the mountain under his powers since the EOs would feel their presence more readily. It would have been a much easier way to travel. Since Hotenfaran knew it would not be safe to walk all night, he would find them a safe place to spend the night before they continued on at sunset.

Serena walked up alongside her uncle and smiled. She knew her uncle was a good man and was doing all he could to ensure their safety but Hotenfaran didn't realize how she and her siblings had become in so short a time. Serena wanted to tell her uncle what they could do but she didn't want him to feel as if she and her siblings did not need him. Serena knew they would need each other more once they got to the cave. It was not going to be an easy feat to accomplish.

Serena decided instead to question Hotenfaran about his Book of Spells and the Invisibility Spell. Her mother and father had both mastered it and had taken it way beyond just making themselves invisible. Serena wanted very much to succeed at this spell before they arrived at their destination. It could be very helpful to Serena so she could get close to her father without anyone seeing her.

"Uncle Hotenfaran, how did you come up with all the spells that you and Mother put into the Book of Spells? Did your parents teach you how to do these things? I am very curious as to how it all came about. I also want to ask you about a particular spell, the Invisibility Spell." Serena eagerly waited for her uncle's answers to her many questions. Her mother did not talk about the book and always changed the subject when Serena had asked her.

"Oh, my dear niece, these spells were passed down through our family for many generations. I don't remember who started to write the spells down. Your mother and I were in the shed, one day, playing with our toys and came across the original book and proceeded to try out some of the spells on each other. We did add the Invisibility Spell with some practice combining other spells. We continued to add our own little spells to the book but the majority of spells are the ones from our ancestors."

Serena listened in awe. She took in every word her uncle said to memory.

"Well, let me tell you what happened when we found the book. Your mother and I got ourselves into big trouble that day because we nearly burned the shed down and the house too using some of the spells. We were punished for a month and didn't get any presents for the holiday season. Your mother still hasn't forgiven me for that time. She had wanted to get a new doll and that year she didn't get anything. By the next year she didn't want it because she was too grown up by that time to play with dolls." He sniggered to himself at the thoughts that were swirling around in his head and the look on his sister's face when the fire had started. Luckily for both of them they got out in time before they were injured in any way. They did manage to quell the fire before it got too bad.

Hotenfaran's thoughts went to his sister. He never would have let anything happen to Solinara; he loved her dearly. He was the older one and had always watched over her when she was little. Queen Solinara didn't need him anymore now that she was a married woman with a family. Hotenfaran felt a little left out and had missed spending time with his sister but then he had met Procelina. They had married and went on the road and had been traveling ever since. He and Procelina, though, missed not having children. But what will be, will be. That was all they could say, for with all their powers they could not make a baby out of thin air.

Hotenfaran heard Serena's voice coming through his memories and he turned his attention back to her. Serena was asking him about the Invisibility Spell.

"Uncle Hotenfaran, I have been studying your book, one spell in particular, the Invisibility Spell. I keep getting stuck on the part where I raise my arm and swing it around in a circle twice then clap my hands together behind my back. Then I say,

"Whirl and swirl,
Make me an invisible girl.
Hide me high and hide me low.
They will never see me; they will never know.
No one will find me no matter where they go."

"When I do this I only half disappear, Uncle Hotenfaran. How do I make my whole self disappear?" Serena's furrowed brow registered just how perplexed she was. As Serena waited for her uncle's reply, she reached into her bag and brought out two Memory Stones her mother had given her and held onto them tightly as their heat began to warm her hands.

Hotenfaran looked kindly at the serious expression registered on Serena's lovely face. He thought Serena looked very much like her mother when she showed this serious side of her personality. Hotenfaran imagined Serena was as strong-willed as her mother and would lock horns with the toughest opponent.

"Well, let me see now. You must concentrate and think of nothing else but the spell. Let us begin at the beginning. First, you raise your right arm up and swing it around in a circle once, twice, then clap your hands behind your back once and recite the spell. Now where did you go, Serena? Are you here?" Hotenfaran looked around and laughed as Serena had disappeared much to her own surprise.

"I did it! Uncle Hotenfaran, I did it! I can't believe it! I have not been able to do it. Thank you so much for your help." Serena, now feeling invincible, hugged him around the neck tightly and placed a noisy kiss on his cheek before bringing herself back from being invisible by reciting the spell backwards.

"You did it all by yourself, my dear niece. You have more power than you let on to me earlier. I am very surprised at your abilities. I was not able to do that spell until I was 19 years old. You are only 14, is that right? Well, you are well on your way to exceeding my powers already.

Does your mother know how talented you are, or are you keeping this from her too?" Hotenfaran looked down at her lovely innocent face. He knew Serena was becoming more and more like her mother all the time. Serena had the same innate sweetness to her and always looked innocent even when she was guilty of something. But he could see how strong willed she could be and determined to do something.

Hotenfaran thought that he was along to lead the group and ensure their safety in completing their mission but now seeing Serena perform one of his toughest spells so expertly, he felt that he really wasn't needed at all. Evidently his sister did not realize just how powerful her oldest daughter was. Hotenfaran thought to himself that if Serena was so powerful; Simon and Catalina must have extensive powers also coming from two powerful people as his sister and her husband.

This prospect made Hotenfaran think about what kind of child Procelina and he would have had. Would their child have had a combination of their powers too? Would their child have been more powerful than they are?

Hotenfaran felt a moment of deep sadness and loss for not experiencing being a father. But he looked over at his two nieces and nephew and felt warmed by the idea of being like a father to them temporarily and having the responsibility of taking care of them until they could find their father.

How would he feel when he didn't have this responsibility anymore? He would have to talk to Procelina about adoption. Hotanfaran had not wanted to talk about it earlier but now he felt as if his life was missing something without children and he was getting older. This is how Procelina must have been feeling all these years. Why was he so blind to her feelings? He would have to make amends and discuss his change of heart with her after they had completed their mission of rescuing his brother-in-law.

This decision brought a smile to Hotenfaran's face and Procelina's too, for she was reading his thoughts from a short distance away. She had been talking with Simon and Catalina when she had noticed Serena's disappearance. She had watched her husband's joy at their niece's success at completing the difficult spell and then the look of sadness that had passed over his face. Hotenfaran seemed so far away in his thoughts that Procelina felt she needed to look into his thoughts to make sure he was all right.

Procelina would not tell Hotenfaran she had done this but she was relieved to know he finally had felt the same emptiness that she had been feeling for years. Procelina had wanted a child and since she could not have one, she wanted to adopt. After this adventure they would talk about the adoption and hopefully find a child who needed them as much as they needed the child. In the meantime, she would not let on that she knew how he was feeling. She would wait until he was ready to tell her for himself.

Procelina smiled and thought, *this trip, though dangerous, will be a turning point for our lives. I only hope that all will end up on the positive side for Gateskin and his family. I will make sure of that.*

PRACTICE MAKES PERFECT

CHAPTER 29

Serena was skipping around and clapping her hands. She was exultant she had finally completed the Invisibility Spell on herself. She now wanted to try it on objects around her.

Simon and Catalina came rushing over to her when they noticed she was so excited. They had seen her standing next to their uncle one minute and the next she had disappeared. They thought that Uncle Hotenfaran had performed the spell on Serena. They had not realized that Serena had done it to herself.

Serena explained to them with so much joy on her face that she glowed. Her eyes sparkled and she had a colorful aura surrounding her like they had never seen before. Simon and Catalina reached forward to touch Serena to see if she was on fire; she was glowing all over. They could feel the electricity emanating off of their sister.

She explained what she had done, "I did it! I did the Invisibility Spell. I can't believe it! Now I want to try it on a rock or maybe a tree." Spindle heard her say something about a tree and came running over.

"Oh Serena, please not a tree!" Spindle pleaded.

"I'm sorry, Spindle. I promise I will not hurt a tree. I only want to make the tree disappear but I promise to bring it back again unharmed."

Spindle nodded his assent and then smiled at her, his face showing much relief. Serena did not want to upset her friend so she used her spell instead on a rock.

Serena waved her hand over a nearby rock and recited the spell.

"Clippity murack, clippity murock,
Make this an invisible rock.
Hide it high and hide it low.
They will never see it; they will never know.
No one will find it no matter where they go."

The rock disappeared and they all looked around in shock that she had done this all by herself. Serena then waved her hand and recited the spell backward and the rock reappeared in the same place.

Catalina was so happy to see the rock back again, that she hopped around and around clapping her hands and laughing. Catalina wanted to do it too just like Serena had done. She looked pleadingly at her sister and asked, "Please, Serena, teach me how to do this."

Catalina had powers of disappearing already anyway but she never knew how she had done it. Catalina just thought about disappearing and then she did. She did not recite a spell or anything else. Also, as a baby Catalina had moved objects with just her mind and blended herself into her surroundings, taking on the color and tone of whatever she thought about. Catalina wanted to be able to control these powers so she could make something disappear and reappear in a more controlled way.

Serena took her sister aside and talked her through the spell and soon she was doing it on her own making trees, birds, and leaves disappear and reappear at will.

Now it was Simon's turn. He could levitate and fly around and move objects with only his mind but wanted to be able to do the spell as his sisters had done. Serena instructed Simon on the fundamental aspects of the spell and soon he was proficient too.

Uncle Hotenfaran and Aunt Procelina stood back and watched their nieces and nephew perform the difficult Invisibility Spell with such ease and proficiency, that the sheer volume of their powers took their breaths away. The children were a formidable threesome and would grow into three of the most powerful fairies and wizard that Hotenfaran and Procelina had ever encountered in their long lives. Even with extensive powers, Hotenfaran and Procelina felt insignificant but knew they had wisdom in age and experience that the children did not possess and this wisdom would be needed in the days ahead to deal with the EOs.

The children settled down after completing the spells and got serious about their mission. They wanted to be prepared to take on anything that came their way in order to rescue their father.

CHAPTER 30

"Well children, are you getting hungry at all?" Hotenfaran asked.

The children jumped up and yelled in unison, "Yes!"

"Procelina, let's spread out the cloth on the ground under that large shady tree and get the packs of food and sit down and partake of the contents. We have some mighty delicious choices here for everyone." Hotenfaran waved his hands over the packs and food flew out to land on the cloth next to them.

The children who had previously been so absorbed in performing spells now rushed over to the tree to sit down and eat. The tantalizing smells coming from their supper were too much for them to resist. They had turkey legs, cole slaw, potato salad and hot rolls that Hotenfaran had conjured up. They even had chocolate cake for dessert. Hotenfaran had prepared a smaller version of the food fit for Spindle to eat. The group ate until they felt sated, laid down and soon the three children and the Sprite were fast asleep.

Procelina and Hotenfaran quickly cleared all the leftover food away and tucked it into the packs for another day. They scanned their surroundings to ensure they were safe and placed an Invisible Enchanted Barrier around them and the children before they too laid down to rest.

A MOTHER WORRIES

CHAPTER 31

Queen Solinara woke up with a start. Her thoughts quickly went to her children and her brother and sister-in-law. Hotenfaran had sent her his latest reports that all was well. "Serena is practicing our Invisibility Spell and had finally mastered it. Serena is an amazing girl." He also spoke highly of Simon and thought Catalina was so sweet and precious.

Queen Solinara smiled to herself at the compliments. She knew how much her brother had wanted children. She was glad he was spending some time with hers and hoped that he would change his mind about adopting one day. Procelina has shared her feelings with Queen Solinara when Hotenfaran had scoffed at the idea of adopting.

Queen Solinara knew they had another day's walk to the cave at the base of Crotesia Mountain. Hotenfaran had told her hey did not want to fly there or they could be spotted more quickly by the EOs guarding the cave so they chose to walk at a steady pace.

Queen Solinara kept her mind open to them so they could keep in touch more easily in case they needed her. She knew her children wanted to do this on their own without her sending her powers to protect them. Queen Solinara knew her brother would take care of the children for her.

King Cavelan and Queen Savina came out to the kitchen where Queen Solinara was now preparing breakfast. They helped her set the tables and called everyone to breakfast as the plates filled with food flew up over their heads and landed at each place setting. The King and Queen knew that everyone needed to eat to restore their strength so they could make their plans for the days to come.

Queen Savina sat next to Queen Solinara and watched as Solinara picked at her food. Savina leaned over to Solinara and whispered, "Solinara, you should try to eat so you can be strong for your husband and children. They may need you at your best."

Solinara smiled and nodded at Queen Savina and thanked her for her concern. "Yes, I know you're right, Savina. I will try to eat a little but my stomach cramps up at the thought of food."

"Yes, I understand, Solinara. I would feel the same if it were my family."

Solinara picked up a forkful of eggs and managed to swallow and took a bite of toast and then sipped her hot brewed chickory coffee.

Solinara had baked the bread that morning, picked the eggs from the chickens' nests, and picked the chickory and ground it just for her guests. All this manual labor kept Solinara busy and her mind active and sane so she didn't have time to worry. Solinara was getting restless and anxious for some word from her husband. Just as she was concentrating on him, Solinara heard a soft knocking at the door to the cottage.

Queen Solinara exchanged looks with Queen Savina and King Cavelan. King Cavelan directed one of his guards, "Go to the door to see who it is."

Queen Solinara, seeing the guard get up, raised her hand to him and headed toward the door alone.

As Queen Solinara got closer, she looked through the peep hole of the door and saw two tiny Sprites standing close together with their hands raised to knock again. She quickly opened the door, startling them, so that they had to step back a few paces before the Sprites could calm themselves down.

Queen Solinara apologized to the Sprites, "Please forgive me for startling you."

The Sprites looked up at her with dazed expressions and nodded.

"What can I do for you? Are you Spindle's parents? He does look like you both."

"Yes, we are, but we are worried Spindle has not returned home since yesterday. Spindle said he was going to visit with his friends, your children, that is. Is he here now? Did he sleep over?" Anabal leaned into Abason and they both looked up at Queen Solinara with worry evident on their little faces.

Queen Solinara knew what that felt like, not knowing if your children were safe or not. She extended her hand in greeting and said, "Please come in and join us for breakfast. We have a lot to talk about. You need not worry about your son. He is safe."

Anabal and Abason exchanged relieved expressions and walked into the cottage to see all the Votovians at the tables eating breakfast. They asked, "Is Spindle here with you?"

"No, he is not here but let me explain."

King Cavelan and Queen Savina got up from the table and set two specially sized places with plates for the Sprites to sit next to Queen Solinara. After they were all seated and had food in front of them, Queen Solinara began to tell Spindle's parents of the adventure her children and Spindle were now on.

Anabal cried softly on her husband's shoulder and Abason gently patted her back to calm her down as he listened intently to Queen Solinara. When Queen Solinara had finished explaining, Abason said, "I know how stubborn and strong-willed Spindle is but I didn't expect him to go on this adventure without telling us."

Abason knew Spindle was a resourceful young man and could take care of himself. He also knew that Spindle was smart and wouldn't do anything to endanger himself or his friends. He knew his son loved Serena and her siblings as if they were part of his own family.

Abason asked Queen Solinara, "If there is anything you need for us to do to help you get your husband back, we will do it without question. We trust our son, Spindle, and know he and your children will come back safely from their adventure. We will send our thoughts to the Sprites along the forest paths to check up on Spindle and your children and to let us know how everyone is and if there is anything they need from us."

Queen Solinara thanked Anabal and Abason and said, "That would be most helpful, Abason. I heard from my brother last night that all was well. I trust my brother and sister-in-law to take care of the children. Please do not worry. I promise to report anything I hear about them." Queen Solinara also said, "I like Spindle. He is a clever boy and very trustworthy."

At this remark Anabal stopped crying, sniffed and then blew her nose and looked over at Queen Solinara and said, "I thank you, Queen Fairy Solinara, for your kindness and hospitality and thoughtful comments about our son. We love him so very much, and as I know you understand, we can't help but be anxious about him until he is safely home again. But we would appreciate hearing anything you can tell us about him to reassure us. Thank you also for sending your brother and sister-in-law to watch over them. This, we greatly appreciate."

The Sprites ate very little and then excused themselves from the table bowing to Queen Solinara, King Cavelan and Queen Savina before leaving the cottage to return to their tree home.

Queen Solinara closed the door behind the Sprites and turned back to her guests as they all exchanged anxious looks. Queen Solinara began to clear the tables with the help of Queen Savina and the other Votovian women as the men went into the extension to continue their plans to ensure the safety of their families.

The children were in the adjoining play area much involved with their toys and were protected by the invisible wall to keep their parents' thoughts from them. The children seemed to be preoccupied with their play and did not seem to be aware of their parents' consternation. But they kept their thoughts open to Serena, Simon and Catalina to find out what was going on. Serena had filled them in to some extent of their adventure but had told them they should stay behind to keep her informed of what the adults were up to.

Serena had told the Votovian children that she and her group were on their way to the cave at the base of the Crotesia Mountain. Serena also told these children of her successful efforts at becoming proficient at performing the Invisibility Spell. This made the Votovian children more in awe of Serena's powers. The Votovian children each had their own powers but none of them were even close to having the abilities that Serena or her brother and sister possessed. This was the reason Serena did not want these children to come along with her for fear of their safety.

DANGERS AHEAD

CHAPTER 32

The dust was blowing around as the adventurers trudged along down the long road. It had not rained in the area for a few months so things were extremely dry and dusty. It made traveling very difficult as each step the group took kicked up more dust. It formed a cloud around them. The rescuers had to keep their cloaks tightly wrapped around their heads and faces in order to keep the dust out of their mouths and noses.

Procelina used her keen hearing and vision to survey the road ahead and area around them for any dangers. It all seemed very quiet indeed. She had noticed that sounds from the birds and insects were absent. This was not a good omen. It meant something was up ahead of them and Procelina put her hand up to the party to signal them to stop and she then sent her thoughts to Hotenfaran that there was something or someone up ahead that could be a danger to them. Procelina thought it could be the EOs guarding the area surrounding the cave. They were, after all, within a few miles of the cave now.

Unbeknownst to the travelers, others were aware of their approach. But luckily these people were not the EOs but the Sprites that could easily hide up in the trees virtually invisible to everyone and everything. The Sprites had received word from Abason, their leader, about his son, Spindle, traveling through the forest on his way to the cave at the base of Crotesia Mountain. The Sprites had promised Abason they would keep an eye on the party of adventurers to ensure their safety and report back to him.

The Sprites whispered back and forth amongst themselves. They flittered from tree to tree following the group. As the group came to an abrupt halt, they in turn did the same.

Procelina suddenly heard the soft whispers and turned around to face the trees. She looked deeply into the trees with her keen vision and spotted the Sprites sitting in bunches in the branches of the trees surrounding them. Procelina now knew that they were not in danger at all from the Sprites. She turned to her husband and said, "All is well. We are not in danger. Let's continue on."

Spindle had suspected something was up when he had heard the familiar whisperings of the Sprites as they passed by the trees. He figured his parents had finally realized he was gone and had found out where from Serena's mother. Spindle knew his father trusted him to be cautious but would do all he could to have the Sprites keep careful watch over him and report back to his father of any problems the party may encounter in their travels.

Spindle couldn't help but smile. He knew his parents loved him very much and would be distraught if something had happened to him. He also knew that if he had told them about this adventure, they would not have let him go. But Spindle had his own agenda besides helping rescue Serena's father; he had planned to look for his uncle who was taken years before. It would make his father very happy to be reunited with his brother after so many years apart. Spindle knew his father had never gotten over the fact that he had lost his brother to the EOs. The EOs had returned to Sovorotskina again over forty years ago and had taken Abason's brother along with some other Sprite children.

The EOs had stumbled upon these children when the Sprites had come out through the woods where the EOs were camped. Micah had fallen out of a tree and the EOs had caught him. A few others were quite young and not fast enough to escape. Abason had earlier flown back up into a tree and out of sight. These Sprites were the only ones the EOs were successful in capturing and bringing back to their village.

PREPARATIONS BEING MADE

CHAPTER 33

Mitteran was reviewing strategies with his troops when one of the guards outside the cave came rushing into his quarters. The Parotovinan was flushed, out of breath, and took a few minutes to compose himself before he began to explain his sudden intrusion upon their meeting.

Mitteran raised his hand to his troops to excuse them because he wanted to speak with the guard alone. Mitteran could tell by the look in the guard's eyes that it was something serious and maybe for his ears alone.

The guard began by apologizing to Mitteran, his superior, "Please excuse my abruptness in entering your quarters, Mitteran."

Mitteran waved his apology away and asked, "What do you want? Why do you need to speak to me?"

The guard replied, "I heard whisperings in the wind that there were troops coming to rescue King Gateskin from the neighboring villages. The whisperings said these troops were in the hundreds. I thought it was necessary to tell you of this news immediately." He bowed his head and averted his eyes from Mitteran as he waited for his response.

"What whisperings? Who told you this? Don't waste my time with such drivel. Get back to your post immediately! I do not want to hear of such things again." Mitteran waved a dismissive hand to the guard who had already turned away and was running out of the cave back to his post. If the intrusive guard had stayed a second longer, he would have seen the anxiety in his superior's eyes over this news.

Mitteran wondered if this was true. Who was whispering to his guard? How many were coming to rescue King Gateskin? Were they prepared to fight his men? Would they be successful? Mitteran thought these questions over and realized he may not succeed on this mission. What would become of his family if he did not bring King Gateskin back to King Kaposkaran?

The only thing Mitteran could do was try to capture more of the villagers and bring them along with King Gateskin to King Kaposkaran. Once Mitteran did this he would then take his family and run as far away as he could from the Land of Darkness and Evil. Mitteran could not do the evil King's bidding anymore. He wanted to live with his family free of all this evil.

It was time to speak with the captive, King Gateskin.

A SECRET IS REVEALED

CHAPTER 34

King Gateskin had just been opening his mind to try to receive his wife's thoughts and those of his friends, the Votovians, when the door to his prison cage suddenly opened. The Staglemite in the cave was preventing him from getting clear messages. They were all jumbled up and he had to decipher them which took a much longer time. King Gateskin finally had figured out Queen Solinara had reported that help was on the way to him - their children and Hotenfaran and Procelina and that he should be alert at all costs to protect himself and the rescuers when they arrived. The thought of anything happening to his children caused a deep pain in King Gateskin's chest and he had to press his hand against it to lessen the pain.

King Gateskin looked up quickly as he sat on a bench against the wall of the cage when Mitteran walked into the room. This cage was near the back of the tunnel of the cave separating the captive from the Head Guard's quarters. King Gateskin wondered what was going on. By the look on Mitteran's face it wasn't something pleasant, he was sure.

Mitteran stood over King Gateskin and cleared his throat before speaking, "King Gateskin, I have come to speak with you about serious matters that must stay private between the two of us. No one must know what I tell you and request from you. Do you understand? If word got out it could mean the death of both of us and our families." Mitteran wore an expression of anxious concern and his brow was deeply creased as he looked at King Gateskin.

King Gateskin at once stood up and reached for Mitteran as he said, "Have you harmed my family in any way? If you did, I will kill you with my bare hands! Do you hear me?" King Gateskin's face turned a brilliant shade of scarlet as his hands tightly fisted in front of him straining the bonds that held him.

Mitteran raised his hands in surrender and motioned for King Gateskin to sit at the table that was in the corner of the room set with two chairs that had been used earlier for King Gateskin's initial interrogation.

After they were both seated, Mitteran waited for King Gateskin to calm down and his face to return to a normal color before beginning his story.

"Please be assured your family is safe. I would not harm them or you. I promise you this. I need your help, King Gateskin. I was serious about this matter being of utmost privacy. I plan to betray my king and it would mean my life if I don't succeed."

Mitteran continued quickly before King Gateskin could interject. "As you know the

Parotovinan King Kaposkaran is not a kind or patient ruler. When he gives an order, a subject must follow it or he will be put to death. If I do not bring some of the children and adult males from the villages to my King, he will kill my family while I watch and then kill me. By that time, I would welcome my death, because not unlike you, I am a family man and love my wife and children more than my own life." Mitteran took a deep breath while he watched his captive's face for any expression of disbelief. He knew that it would be hard to convince King Gateskin of what he planned to do. He couldn't believe he was going to do it, either.

"Do you expect me to believe that you would go against your own king? What do you expect me to say? I am a doomed man either way."

"I don't expect you to believe me as a Parotovinan subject, but maybe as a fellow Sovorotskinan, descendant of Noella I."

King Gateskin's face again changed color but this time it was white as chalk from Mitteran's shocking revelation.

CLOSING IN

CHAPTER 35

The guard at the mouth of the cave returned to his post to sulk and fret over what he had done. He knew he shouldn't have disturbed Head Guard, Mitteran. Now he would never be considered seriously for a promotion. He knew he had acted hastily. But the voices were getting louder and more persistent. It had to be a warning. The guard felt his hands shaking as he listened to the loud whisperings. He felt as if he were going insane as he clamped his hands tightly over his ears to soften the whispers.

The Sprites watched over the opening of the cave and closely observed the anxious guard. They had been directing their whispers toward him only. The other guards were unaware of anything going on. The Sprites wanted to discredit this guard so that no one would believe him when the rescuers actually arrived. It would give the rescuers some much needed time and the element of surprise in order to be successful in their rescue of King Gateskin.

The travelers needed all the help they could get. They had no idea the help they would receive would be from some that were so small, yet quite powerful in number.

The guard collapsed in exhaustion by a tree near the cave entrance. He decided to contact his village wizards to tell them about this new development. He waited for a response.

***

Back in Parotovina, the wizards met to discuss the message received by the guard. They were hesitant to inform the King just yet. For if they were wrong, he would surely execute them for false information.

They decided to tell the guard, "Stay at the cave entrance and keep your eyes and ears open for further developments. If you actually see these rescuers, inform us right away and hold your position until we tell you otherwise."

The guard nodded as the message reached his mind. He sent back. "I am not moving from the cave until you tell me otherwise." He further promised, "I will stay alert for any rescuers coming this way."

This guard was known to make up stories and imagine he was a hero in his eyes only. He was known as a braggart, always trying to gain favor from King Kaposkaran.

This fact was fortunate for the rescuers who were almost there and this may have saved their lives.

CHAPTER 36

The party was getting closer to Crotesia Mountain, Hotenfaran noted, as the terrain began to get rockier and rougher. Hotenfaran slowed down and made eye contact with Procelina. "Can we continue on without being attacked. There are guards posted at the cave." Hotenfaran knew Procelina's hearing was exemplary and she would alert him of any sounds that he could not hear.

Procelina nodded to Hotenfaran and whispered, "All is quiet." She then gathered the children together to tell them, "From now on we must travel without talking." Procelina would put a protective spell over them all to keep them together and make them invisible to the guards so the rescuers could get as close as possible to the cave without being detected. Procelina had planned to go into the cave alone once they got there to find King Gateskin. She wanted to keep the children safe from harm. Procelina had promised Queen Solinara she would do this and she always kept her promises.

The travelers did not know what was transpiring within the cave between Gateskin and the Head Guard, Mitteran. If they had known, they may have taken another path and planned something different in their rescue attempts.

CHAPTER 37

"I can't believe what you are saying to me? You could be trying to trick me into helping you, then you will kill me and my family just to ensure your own life and the lives of your family." King Gateskin's face was still white but his eyes showed a fierceness that Mitteran had seen before of a man who is desperate and would do anything to save his family.

"No, please King Gateskin, believe me. This is the truth. I have lived all my life in Parotovina but my mother told me of a different life that her parents had when they lived in Sovorotskina. They said it was a beautiful land of light and plenty. Everyone got along and there was no evil ruler. They worked in their gardens and worshiped as they pleased and raised their families in peace and love."

"That is the life I want for my family. My children live in fear of their lives each day they go to school. In the schools they teach all the children of evil and of killing all those who are not from Pavorotskina. My children are good and kind and I do not want them to become evil as our ruler one day. I want them to run free in the fields and laugh and be happy. I want that for myself too! I am sick of all the evil deeds I have had to carry out. I pray that god and goddess Ramoforan and Ressaphena will forgive me and my transgressions one day! I want to be free to live where I choose with my family as you do. Please help me!" Mitteran hung his head and covered his face with his hands as his shoulders shook and tears ran down his face through his fingers to drop onto the table in front of him.

King Gateskin reached forward with his bound hands to offer Mitteran comfort and support. When King Gateskin's bound hands pressed

Mitteran's shoulder he looked up at King Gateskin.

"I believe you, my friend. What can I do to help? Will you guarantee my family's safety at all costs?" King Gateskin looked intently at Mitteran, his eyes still showing the fierce determination he felt.

"I will do all that I can to ensure your safety and that of your family. We must make our plans now. I know there are many of your people coming this way now to attempt to rescue you. My guard told me he heard whisperings of a large contingency heading this way. I do not want any of them injured, so we must meet them together before they reach the cave. I will give you up to them and tell my men it is a trap to capture all of your people and bring them back to King Kaposkaran. They will believe me since I am their leader."

King Gateskin let out a gasp of shock as he listened to Mitteran. He looked closely at the Head Guard and said, "I must tell you something now, Mitteran. The people that are coming this way to rescue me are none other than my children led by my brother-in-law and his wife. They must be kept safe or I will kill anyone that even threatens them in any way." King Gateskin's eyes turned a glowing shade of gold as he spoke these words.

"You mean to tell me your children are coming to rescue you with only their uncle and aunt for protection? Why, they are too young to do this! They could be killed by my guards! How could you let them do this?" Mitteran looked at King Gateskin in disbelief.

"I know they are just babies but you do not know my children, especially my oldest, Serena, who is 14. She is very headstrong like her mother and would not listen to reason. Her mother tried to talk her out of it, but when she couldn't, Solinara contacted her brother Hotenfaran and his wife, Procelina, to accompany the children to ensure their safety. They are very powerful as a wizard and fairy go. Also, my children have their own powers that will one day be formidable as they hone them and gain experience." King Gateskin smiled with love and pride at the thought of his children coming to his rescue. He did fear for their safety but trusted Hotenfaran and

Procelina to keep them safe or they would have to account to him.

"You must have remarkable children for them to take on this enormous task. They must love you greatly! Did you say that they are the only ones coming for you with their uncle and aunt? You have three children, is that correct, King Gateskin? Three plus your brother-in-law and his wife makes only five rescuers. How did they expect to overpower my guards?" Mitteran just shook his head and looked at King Gateskin incredulously.

"Ah, yes, though there may only be five coming to my rescue, they are all very powerful indeed, let me assure you. This is not coming from a proud father but from a learned one. I have seen what they can do with their young powers. Believe me they have nearly as much power as I have. They just need more experience and practice; that is all. They can only get stronger with time."

"My guard told me recently about whispers of a large rescue party that was coming for you. I knew the guard was not imagining the whispers. But I think you may have more help than you expected. The whispers my guard heard, I am sure, came from the Sprites. They are not usually involved in anything other than if their own lives were in danger. You must have done something to gain their favor."

Mitteran knew of the Sprites from stories he had heard as a child. He had never actually seen one but there were many interesting stories about the feats of such fascinating and elusive little creatures. The stories became more and more fantastic as they were passed on to each generation. Mitteran also knew that they were the ones to pass on his message to King Gateskin, as he had hoped. This was probably why they were following King Gateskin to watch over him and report back to King Gateskin's family.

King Gateskin explained, "The Sprites, are friends of all the villagers. We help one another to survive and live in peace from you and..." King Gateskin stopped before he could say something he may regret later on. After all, King Gateskin thought, Mitteran seemed like a decent family man like himself. He had finally been honest and straightforward with him about his background. Mitteran may even be related to him and the other villagers from Sovorotskina and Votovia. King Gateskin would have to trust Mitteran with his own life and that of his children. Gateskin only hoped and prayed he would not regret this decision. But, what other choice did he have? Maybe it was time to be honest with Mitteran too. Things seemed to be falling into place for both of them. If they joined forces, they just might be successful to save each other and their families too.

Mitteran leaned across the table, took a key out of his pocket and unlatched the chain binding King Gateskin's wrists together, he patted King Gateskin on the back.

King Gateskin rubbed his sore wrists to get the stiffness out of them and then extended his hand to Mitteran in truce and friendship. Mitteran in turn shook King Gateskin's hand firmly.

King Gateskin looked solemnly at Mitteran and said, "It is my turn now to be honest with you. I had planned to meet with you prior to your scheduling the meeting in the forest. I, too, wanted to ask you to betray your king and help me save my family and the villages. I never realized you felt so strongly about leaving your land or that you were a fellow Sovorotskinan. I will do whatever it takes to save our families and keep King Kaposkaran from obtaining any more TOs."

"Well, my friend, it looks like we have surprised each other with our plans. I think we will be able to work out something so we can both be happy and keep our families safe," Mitteran exclaimed.

"Will your men support you if you tell them what you plan to do? Or, will we do this behind their backs keeping them in the dark?" King Gateskin inquired, feeling somewhat better about the current situation. A short time earlier it had seemed dire indeed.

Mitteran sadly shook his head. "There are many good men in my command but there are a few who are loyal to our King and cannot be trusted to support us in any way. In fact, they have been known to spy on me and they do report back to King Kaposkaran daily on the progress of our mission. The King knows now that we have you in our control and he is waiting for word of when we will return. He also expects us to bring back many villagers too. As long as we are in this cave, he cannot hear our plans thanks to the Staglemite in the walls. I am sure you have noticed this and have had a hard time getting messages from your wife and the men under your command."

"Yes, but I have managed with some difficulty to decipher part of the messages sent to me. For the missing parts I tried to fill in the blanks to make sense of the messages. Hopefully I am filling in the blanks correctly."

"You are cleverer than I, for I have not been able to decipher any messages that the King or my family have been sending to me. I must leave the cave nightly and sit outside in the woods to send out my messages to allay my wife's fears for my safety. The ones I send to the King are just to assure him that I am fulfilling my duties."

King Gateskin nodded to Mitteran, "I understand now what has to be done," and listened intently as Mitteran proceeded to describe the plan he had in mind to trick his own men in order to save King Gateskin and his family of rescuers heading their way.

Now if it all worked out...

HELP IS NEAR

CHAPTER 38

"Spindle, can I speak to you a minute?" Procelina led Spindle off the path out of the hearing of the rest of the group. She wanted to ask Spindle some questions but did not want the other children to hear the answers.

"Of course, Procelina, what is it? Did I do something wrong? I thought I was walking as fast as I could." Spindle had a frightened look in his eyes as he looked up at Procelina with her crown of hair flying all around her face. He did not want to anger her for fear of what she would look like if she were angry. She was quite a sight as it was when she was calm as she was at the moment.

"Oh, little one, I didn't mean to frighten you so. I am not angry at you. You are doing just fine. I am surprised how fast you can walk on such little legs. I just wanted to ask you why your Sprite friends are whispering so frantically. Is there something you need to tell me that I should know in order to protect us on our journey? There are many dangers ahead, and I need for you to be honest with me. It could mean our lives. Do you understand, Spindle?"

"I…. ah…I don't know what they are up to. They may be taking orders from my father. He is Head of the Council of Elders. He also has control of the Sprite army in times of danger of impending war. Not that we have ever had a war or had to fight in that way. We usually just use our minds to control situations to prevent any danger to ourselves. I guess they are doing that in some way. Maybe…" Spindle stopped talking and looked toward the trees and listened.

Procelina perked up her ears and did the same. She heard the whispers getting louder and more distinct. They were all around them as if they were in a tunnel of sound, each whisper reverberating back and forth.

Procelina turned to Spindle and in her own whisper, "I think they are trying to tell us something very important. Spindle, you may need to interpret for me what they are saying. I can hear them but don't understand the language they are using."

"It is the old language. They only use the old language when they are agitated, frightened or excited about something. They are saying that there was a meeting in the cave between the Head Guard and King Gateskin but they could not hear what was being said. They could not get into the cave without endangering themselves or the King. They also said that they were successful in driving the main guard at the mouth of the cave crazy with their whisperings so they could discredit him when we arrived. They wanted to give us some much-needed time to rescue the King without any harm coming to any of us. They are now concentrating their whisperings on the other guards at the back of the cave to distract them away from the cave giving us access to it."

"My, oh my, they are a clever lot, aren't they though? Who would have thought the smallest creatures would be the most successful at diversion! I guess we won't have to create a diversion since they are taking care of that part of the rescue. We can concentrate on getting into the cave and getting King Gateskin out of there."

Spindle gurgled and nodded. "Yes, I guess we are clever little Sprites."

"Can you give them a message for me, Spindle? Can you tell them that we appreciate all the help they can give us to keep up the diversion so we can get into the cave? We will go by the back entrance, see if they can thoroughly distract the guards from that part of the cave. Ok?" Procelina's brain was whirling and she was thoroughly in her zone. She felt now they had a very good chance to succeed.

Procelina went back to the rest of the group and sent her thoughts to Hotenfaran and he smiled back at her and winked his eye in agreement and relief. Procelina could tell that Hotenfaran had been worried over how they were going to get into the cave on their own. Now they had a plan and friends to back them up. They were no longer alone. It was nice to have help regardless of the size of the support.

LOVE IS IN THE AIR

CHAPTER 39

Serena, Simon and Catalina exchanged knowing looks and thoughts. They could tell from the brief meeting along the path between Procelina and Spindle that something was up. Procelina had kept her mind and thoughts closed to them but now the channel was open and Serena could invade these thoughts. Serena felt a little guilty doing so, but knew it had to be done to ensure the safety of her siblings. She needed to know what was going on so she could help. Serena knew that she would always have to prove herself until she reached the age when her powers would be at their peak.

Serena decided the best thing to do was to speak with Spindle about his Sprite friends. She knew her mother had something to do with this also. Serena knew that Queen Solinara was being kept up-to-date by her aunt and uncle and the Sprites under the leadership of Spindle's father, Abason. Serena wondered if everyone realized that she could take care of them all by herself. Serena walked off in a huff to speak with Spindle. She would just have to show them how powerful she could be when times got tough.

Spindle was walking alongside Procelina when he spotted Serena coming toward him in a hurry. He could tell by the determined look on her face that it was not going to be good news. Spindle cringed to himself and tried to shake off the feeling of dread and the fact that he was going to have to deal with Serena and her temper. Spindle knew Serena would ask him what Procelina said to him in private whispers and why Serena had not been privy to their conversation.

Before he could come to a decision about how to deal with Serena she stopped a few inches from him, kneeled down in front of Spindle to get at his level and stared into his eyes. Serena's eyes were so beautiful, Spindle thought, even when she was angry. Her eyes seemed to have flecks of gold in them and shot off sparks like fireflies darting to and fro in the night.

"Spindle, I need to talk to you," Serena said in a soft, sweet voice belaying the steely look in her eyes.

"Ah, yes, I…oh, what do you want to talk about, Serena?" Spindle stuttered as he felt his face flush from her staring at him so intently.

"Is there something you would like to share with me, Spindle?" Serena said so sweetly that Spindle thought he might have imagined she was angry with him. Spindle averted his eyes from Serena's before he answered.

"What…what do you mean? I don't have anything to tell you." Spindle could not look Serena in the eye for she would know that he was lying if she didn't already know that fact.

"Well, I beg to differ. Now, fess up, my friend. Remember that this adventure was my idea and I am still in charge of you and my siblings. You take my lead not my aunt's or uncle's. Do you understand?" Serena's voice now had icicles of frost in it.

"Yes...of course. I am here for you at your beck and call and to aid you in any way that I can. I promised your mother I would keep you and your siblings safe. Queen Solinara promised me a gooseberry pie if I brought you all back unharmed. You know how much I love your mother's gooseberry pie! You saw me sneak a few bites that day. I know you did. But why didn't you tell your mother when she asked if you saw anyone do it?" Spindle was very good at changing the subject when he was in trouble or if he felt cornered.

"Spindle, are you listening to me? Stop changing the subject." Serena tried to keep her voice sharp but couldn't help but smile when she thought back to that summer when she first saw Spindle at the window leaning over the pie and thoroughly enjoying each tiny bite. Serena did not have the heart to stop Spindle or to squeal on him to her mother. Even though

Serena found out later on that her mother knew Spindle had been the culprit.

"Well, yes, I did see you eating the pie but I figured your bites were so small that my mother may not have even noticed the indentation in the pie. I really don't think she minded even though she tried to make her voice angry when she asked me if I knew who had done it."

Spindle smiled back at Serena as he thought over that day when he had his first close glimpse of beautiful Serena. Just seeing her looking back at him with her incredible eyes, he had lost his appetite for the pie and had run away. Spindle would never forget Serena's translucent face and her colorful aura. That was the day he fell in love with her. As he looked at her now, he felt the same pull in his chest as his heart beat faster.

"Are you listening to me, Spindle?" Serena said as she reached forward and touched his arm to bring him out of his daydream.

The Sprite felt the electric current run through his arm at her touch. "Oh... I am so sorry, Serena. I was just thinking about that day. Do you know that was the first time I saw you up close? I was a little nervous about getting too close. I wasn't sure if you would try to harm me. But now I see that you are a kind and true friend to me and would never ever think of harming me in any way. Even if you were angry with me, right, Serena?" Spindle gave Serena his most beautiful smile then hung his head down so as not to meet her eyes.

Serena could not help herself and let out a hearty laugh at her small friend's conniving ways. Spindle certainly knew how to get around her and get her out of a funk and into a good mood again. Spindle also had the talent to make her forget what she was angry with him about.

"Oh Spindle, you are too much but you know you always make me feel good even when I am angry with you. I can't stay angry very long. What I wanted to ask you was about your meeting with my Aunt Procelina. What did she say to you? Is it something I need to know? Now be honest with me, please. I am not angry with you, I promise. I just need to know everything. We are so close now to my father. I can feel his presence. It is getting stronger."

"I can understand how you feel, Serena. Your aunt had asked me about the Sprites. Procelina could hear the whispers but could not understand the language that they were speaking. She asked me to interpret the messages for her. The Sprites were whispering to the guards to try to distract them from our presence and aid us in getting into the cave to rescue your father. The Sprites have been in constant contact with my father and he in turn with your mother."

"I see, now I understand why she took you aside. Thank you for your help and for being here with us. I appreciate your assistance. You did not have to do this. Your life could be in danger too. You are a true friend, Spindle. I lo...like you very much, you know that." Serena turned and walked away quickly before Spindle could see the rosy flush on her cheeks as she almost said the 'L' word to him. She didn't know what came over her. How could she do that? He would think she was crazy! How could a Fairy love a Sprite? Did she really love him or was she overreacting to his support?

Spindle was left standing there with his mouth open. Did Serena almost say the 'L' word to him? *Wow, can it be possible she loves me too?* Spindle thought, *this had to be the best day of my life!* He found himself skipping along to catch up with the rest of the group feeling very happy and content in spite of what dangers they may be facing ahead.

A TIME TO REGROUP

CHAPTER 40

Hotenfaran listened intently to his sister's thoughts as Queen Solinara explained about the Staglemite in the cave interfering with her thought transfers between her and King Gateskin. "I know you can come up with a solution to the problem, Hotenfaran. You always have." Queen Solinara knew her brother would come up with the solution to a problem whenever she asked him for help.

Queen Solinara had not depended upon Hotenfaran for a long time after she married King Gateskin. Her husband had taken over as the problem solver in the family. Queen Solinara realized now why Hotenfaran had distanced himself since their marriage. She must make it up to Hotenfaran somehow for how she had tossed him aside so carelessly.

Hotenfaran smiled to himself, their thoughts flying back and forth, as his sister apologized for not showing her appreciation for all his talents and taking him for granted. Queen Solinara confessed, "I have missed you, Hotenfaran and of course love you dearly. After this adventure we will have to spend some time bonding again as brother and sister."

Hotenfaran agreed, "I have missed you too. I agree, Solinara. We need to spend more time together and develop some new spells to put into the Book of Spells for all eternity."

Hotenfaran wanted to put in some new ones to challenge his niece, Serena. Serena had been working hard on several of the toughest spells in the book and had almost mastered them already. He told Queen Solinara, "I can't believe how talented and powerful Serena is. I had to chuckle at the sight of Serena as she spun herself around chanting the spells and the joy expressed in her face as Serena mastered yet another spell on their journey."

As Queen Solinara received his thoughts, they made her smile with pride too. She knew her eldest daughter was very powerful indeed. "Yes, she is quite powerful for someone so young." This fact made Queen Solinara relax a little as she thought how far away her children were now and that she could not be with them all. But she knew in her mind and her heart Hotenfaran and Procelina would keep their promise to her and bring them back safely along with her husband. Queen Solinara looked forward with great pleasure to their reunion. Until then, there was still much to do. She would keep sending her thoughts and powers their way.

Hotenfaran told Solinara, "I will work on a solution to the Staglemite interference and I assure you I will take care of it very soon."

"Thank you, brother." Solinara said and signed off so Hotenfaran could continue on his journey and give all his attention to the children and their rescue plan.

CHAPTER 41

Hotenfaran and Procelina brought the children together in a tight group to finalize their plan for the rescue of King Gateskin. Their young faces were innocent but showed an eagerness and strength that they would need in the next several hours. They were nearing the mouth of the cave and Hotenfaran had spread a new Invisible Curtain Spell over the group to keep them safe from the guards who they could now see in the distance at the cave.

There were several guards bordering the mouth of the cave and also stationed at the other end.

The Sprites had reported that one of the guards was sleeping at the back of the cave and another one was very bored and soon would be joining his fellow guard in slumber. The Sprites were no longer whispering but singing in a calming manner in order to help the guards along to sleep.

The group looked at one another and all nodded in agreement as they moved forward in tight formation three by three. Three of them would go to the mouth of the cave, Procelina, because of her acute hearing, along with Simon and holding tightly to her brother's hand, Catalina. Simon gave Catalina's hand a reassuring squeeze as they moved slowly under the Invisible Curtain Spell toward the cave.

In the meantime, the other three, Hotenfaran, Serena, and bringing up the rear, was Spindle carefully corresponding with his fellow Sprites who were watching the guards around the cave from the border of the trees.

HELP IS NEAR!

CHAPTER 42

"It is time, King Gateskin. Let me bind your hands again before we go out of the cave. I will keep you ahead of me with my sword at your back. Walk slowly and do as I say once we reach the guards. I don't want them to be suspicious of our movements." Mitteran looked somewhat anxious but determined to make their plan work.

King Gateskin nodded at Mitteran, moved ahead of him and slowly walked forward down the dark corridors to the mouth of the cave. King Gateskin could see the guard's back as the guard stood very straight and tall outside the opening of the cave. The guard's ears seemed to perk up as he heard the crunch under the duo's feet as they approached him. The guard quickly turned to face King Gateskin and Mitteran, alert and ready to defend his commander if need be.

Mitteran raised his hand to the guard and whispered to him, "All is well. Stay here. I am going to take the prisoner out to the forest to meet the rescuers who you reported were on their way to the cave to make a deal with them."

Mitteran instructed the guard further, "You must stay behind to keep watch until I return. I will call if I need you."

The guard didn't look quite convinced that his commander would be safe unless he could accompany him on this mission. But the guard stood steadfast in his promise to their King that he would follow the Head Guard's word at all times.

Mitteran couldn't help but smile at the guard who looked thoroughly confused and torn at what to do. The guard's fear of retribution from their King was the only thing keeping him at his post.

Mitteran kept his sword pointed at King Gateskin's back for the benefit of the other guards around the cave as he moved King Gateskin forward toward the path in the forest leading them to the rescuers.

Unbeknownst to either party, they would pass one another very closely, for seconds after the two left the cave, the three rescuers entered it finding it abandoned. The rescuers were very puzzled over what could have happened to King Gateskin and the Head Guard, Mitteran. The Staglemite must have rubbed off onto King Gateskin's clothes obliterating the movements of both King Gateskin and Mitteran and their conversation so that Procelina could not pick the sounds up.

Procelina listened carefully as the three of them were leaving the cave and then heard the guard at the mouth whispering to the other guards and relaying what had just transpired between the guard and Mitteran. The other guards looked confused too and wondered what was going on. A couple of them were more brazen than others and decided to go out to the forest to find out what their commander was doing.

Procelina brought her finger up to her lips and sent her thoughts to the rest of the group that they were a little late in getting to King Gateskin. The rescuers' plan was now changed and they were to meet on the path out in the woods once again.

Mitteran spoke to King Gateskin once he knew they were out of earshot of his guards. As Mitteran looked around them, he asked King Gateskin, "Where are the rescuers. Are you sure they are coming?"

"Yes, they are sending me a message now."

King Gateskin opened his mind and picked up signals from his daughter, Serena, that she was coming his way. Serena said she was looking in the cave for him and must have just missed him. Serena told her father to stay where he was and that the group would be there shortly. King Gateskin smiled at the thought of seeing his children again but he knew the danger was not over just yet until he could get them back home safely.

Hotenfaran and his two companions met the other three on the path entering the forest. Procelina exchanged looks with Hotenfaran and they nodded at one another. Procelina rewove the Invisible Curtain Spell with a wave of her hand encompassing the whole group for safety. Procelina could hear the guards approaching behind them.

Spindle sent messages to his fellow Sprites to tell them that they needed assistance to distract the guards so the rescuers could get to King Gateskin unharmed.

A great booming sound was suddenly heard in the distance beyond the group as they ventured into the forest. The group of rescuers stopped to listen but kept closely knit as they walked on. Spindle was seen smiling broadly and nodded at Serena as she almost laughed out loud. Serena then smiled at her uncle and aunt who were also grinning after reading Serena's thoughts.

The guards, who were behind the group, were so startled by the loud boom that they dropped their swords, turned and ran all the way back to the cave to find that the rest of the guards had disappeared.

The rescuers, much relieved, moved more quickly to meet with King Gateskin and the Head Guard. They were still not sure of what they would find and why the Head Guard, Mitteran, had taken King Gateskin out to the forest. What did Mitteran plan to do to King Gateskin? Why did Mitteran venture out alone with his prisoner?

Serena looked up ahead and along with her siblings spotted their father and ran to meet him. They noticed the Head Guard standing off to the side of the path giving them room to move forward. Mitteran had quickly unbound Gateskin's hands as his children rushed forward.

Serena read her father's thoughts and could see a serenity and peace in his facial expressions that there was nothing to fear of Mitteran. The group was released from the Invisible Curtain Spell by Procelina, unimpeded yet vulnerable.

The three children surrounded their father with whoops and hollers of joy as they hugged and kissed him. He laughed out loud with relief and happiness at their boisterousness. "Well, I am relieved that you are all safe."

Hotenfaran and Procelina stepped forward with Spindle to meet King Gateskin. They had noticed King Gateskin's hands were not bound and that Mitteran had shouldered his sword in its scabbard.

King Gateskin stepped forward to offer his hand to Hotenfaran. He patted him heartily on the back as he hugged him tightly as he said, "I don't know how to thank you both." He leaned over to kiss Procelina on each cheek and hugged her too. King Gateskin gently shook Spindle's little hand and gave him a wink and sent him thoughts and thanks for his help and that of the other Sprites.

"The booming sound came from the Sprites as they all knocked on the trees at the same time – thousands of them," Spindle related to King Gateskin.

King Gateskin's handsome face showed his relief and joy at being reunited with his children. But suddenly his face became very serious as he looked at Mitteran. It was time to let everyone in on their plan, King Gateskin thought. He looked at his rescuers and said, "I am deeply indebted to you all. You are very brave to have come all this way for me. Now it is my turn to keep you safe and take you home."

"You must all be wondering why we are out here instead of in the cave. Mitteran, do you want me to tell them or do you?" King Gateskin looked kindly at Mitteran as the Head Guard came forward to meet the group.

"You have a wonderful family, King Gateskin. Your children are very brave indeed and beautiful and handsome just like their parents." Mitteran shook each rescuer's hand in turn before continuing.

"I think I need to tell you all something very important. Procelina, would you do me a favor and put us all under a spell to keep what I need to tell you just amongst us here? I know how powerful and effective your spells are. You are known as a very great fairy back in Parotovina."

287

This is all Procelina needed to hear, that she was famous even in the Land of Evil and Darkness. Procelina looked over at her husband and winked and before they knew it Procelina had raised her hands and with the aid of Hotenfaran had spread a Staglemite curtain over all of them. This spell Hotenfaran had just conjured up with a little stolen Staglemite from the cave. Hotenfaran had promised his sister he would get to the bottom of the Staglemite problem. He did it now by using it in a more productive way against their enemies.

"Thank you, my new friends, for this. Well, I should begin at the beginning. After all, we have some time now since all my guards have run away and may never come back this way again." Mitteran grinned at the group.

This statement made all of them laugh out loud with relief. But they quickly looked serious again when Mitteran began his tale.

"As you know, many years ago the EOs came into the villages and took many Taken Ones or TOs back to their village of Parotovina. I have lived there all my life and have a family of my own now. But what you don't know is that my parents told me stories of another village called Sovorotskina where their parents had once lived. This makes me a descendant of the TOs."

The group let out an audible gasp at this news. They were now looking not upon an enemy but now a friend and possibly a relative from their own beloved village of Sovorotskina. They stepped forward to embrace Mitteran but he held up his hand to them to let him finish his tale.

"I have wanted to leave this evil village of Parotovina for as long as I can remember as a child. We have been waiting for someone to help us escape. There were many people over the years from the others' villages who tried to rescue my grandparents and other TOs but they were captured and killed by the King. My grandparents kept a list of all the TOs and what villages they came from. All the descendants of the TOs have copies of this scroll. We keep adding our names and then passing it on to our children. We must never forget or be forgotten." Mitteran covered his face with his hands and shook his head as he tried to compose himself to go on.

"My family is in danger now that I have taken it upon myself to release King Gateskin and refuse to do any more of King Kaposkaran's evil deeds. I only ask of King Gateskin that he help me get my family out of Parotovina safely. The only way I can do this is by taking him back with me along with two of you. I do not want to take the children, but I would appreciate it if Hotenfaran and Procelina would come back with me. We can work something out to protect you all. I know how powerful you both are. I cannot do this alone. I know this is a lot to ask of you. I will understand if you refuse to help. I will have to do what I can on my own to save my family." Mitteran's face had turned green as he looked as if he would be sick.

Hotenfaran and Procelina exchanged looks and walked toward Mitteran and wrapped him in a double embrace. They both spoke as one, "We will do whatever is necessary, Mitteran, to aid you in getting your family out of the grip of King Kaposkaran. We know enough spells to distract the guards in the village so you can go to your home and hide your family from the King. We could use the Invisibility Spell and I have a few tricks up my sleeve, eh, Procelina?"

He smiled lovingly at his wife who returned his devoted gaze.

Serena spoke up immediately so as not to be excluded from this new adventure. She said with much enthusiasm, "Uncle Hotenfaran, I can handle the Invisibility Spell for you. As you know, I have mastered it along with several of the other spells from your Book of Spells." Her face glowed and she thrust her chin defiantly upward as she looked at the adults who were now staring at her with wide-eyed expressions.

Hotenfaran nodded at Serena but let King Gateskin intercede.

"Oh, my dear darling daughter, Serena, I cannot allow you to endanger yourself. After all, I was going to entrust you with the care of your siblings in getting them back home safely. I am sure that Spindle will assist you in doing just that." King Gateskin looked at his lovely daughter with consternation apparent in his eyes. He knew it was almost hopeless to expect her to do as she was told.

"I am sorry, Father, but I must insist that I be allowed to go on this journey to help our friend and fellow Sovorotskinan, Mitteran, rescue his family from the evil King Kaposkaran. After this mission is accomplished, I promise to take my brother and sister back home to Mother. I sent her word we are all safe and that we will not be home just yet; but that we have another rescue to make first. She reluctantly agreed to allow me to complete this new mission as long as you agreed also." Serena looked adoringly at her father's once tanned and rugged face which was now very pale with this news.

"Serena, you are surely too much like your mother in temperament. She always gets her way with me!" King Gateskin was feeling like he was being used by both his daughter and wife with their wily ways. He couldn't help it but found himself laughing at the prospect of a man who was so in control of everything around him except the women in his life. As he was laughing over this, he looked down to see his youngest daughter, Catalina, tugging at his pant leg to get his attention.

He got down on one knee to get closer to Catalina to see what she wanted to tell him. Catalina smiled her sweetest smile at her father before beginning to tell him what was so important to her at that moment.

"Father, I am a big girl and I want to help rescue Mitteran's family too! I can do some spells almost as good as Serena. Please, Father, let me go too! I can even disappear like this...now you can't see me!" Before his very eyes, Catalina performed the Invisibility Spell and disappeared to reappear behind her father much to his surprise.

"Well, I can see you are very powerful for a little girl. I don't see how I can refuse you at this point, can I?" Before he could continue, Catalina had hopped up onto his back and was laughing and hugging him fiercely around the neck.

"Now, does this mean that I can go too, Father?" Simon was now by his side looking up into his father's eyes. "I am powerful too, Father. I can perform many of the spells in Uncle Hotenfaran's book too. Do you want to see me do one for you now?" Simon was anxiously waiting for his father to just say the word and he was ready to perform.

"No, it is quite all right, my son. You can go on this adventure but you must all promise me that you will do what I tell you to do and when I tell you to do it. I cannot jeopardize your safety in any way. I am responsible for all of you now, not the other way around." His face became very serious and his eyes were like steel. When he looked like this, his children knew there was nothing else to do but say 'yes Father.' They all responded in kind. They listened then to what they were to do on this new journey into the Land of Darkness.

Serena noticed that Spindle, who was standing along the tree line away from the rest of the group, was very quiet through all this; but it was because he was conferring with the Sprites about the new journey they were about to begin. The Sprites were in the process of reassuring Spindle that they would inform his father of this change of plans and they promised to keep close by in case they were again needed when Serena came up to Spindle to ask him if he was all right. Spindle nodded his thanks at the Sprites before directing his full attention to Serena. Spindle smiled at her and felt himself get warm all over just having her stand so close to him. Serena was truly more beautiful every time he looked at her.

"Spindle, did you hear me? I asked you if you are all right." Serena looked at Spindle's handsome, smiling face and couldn't help but smile right back at him. Spindle could always do that to her. He was incorrigible, she thought! She felt herself forgetting once again what she was going to say to him. Serena's face showed her consternation and exasperation at her own ineptitude.

"What did you say, Serena? Did you ask me if I was all right? Of course, I am just *green*! I was so involved, in conference with the Sprites, that I didn't quite hear you at first. They will be informing my father of our plans and they also promised to keep a watch over us in case we need their assistance again. The Sprites were pretty clever back there, don't you think, for little creatures? I never knew Sprites could make so much noise! I guess since there are so many of us, anything is possible!" Spindle laughed his funny tinkling laugh that always made Serena laugh too.

"Hey, you two! What are you conspiring to do? There better not be anymore funny business from the Sprites. That noise they made nearly made me drop dead from shock!" Hotenfaran said with a definite gleam in his eyes showing a newfound respect for the little Sprites and their amazing abilities and ingenuity. The Sprites were definitely important allies to have on one's side when things got tough.

Spindle skipped his way over to the grownups and reassured them. "Don't worry, I can keep my Sprite friends in line if need be."

A whistling sound could be heard that soon surrounded them. Spindle looked in the direction of the trees and bowed his head and shook it back and forth looking somewhat chagrined and chastised by the Sprites for his remark. The sound soon dissipated down to a soft hiss. The Sprites had made their point known who was in charge here. It certainly wasn't Spindle. They had more than proven they could take care of themselves and the rest of the group without lifting a finger. A chuckling sound soon was heard all through the forest that grew louder and louder and reverberated back and forth until it finally faded away.

"Thank you, my dear little friends, for all that you have done for us. We truly could not have survived to get this far without you. We are indebted to you forever, I fear. I will be at your service if you ever need a wizard after this adventure is over. Please let me know." Hotenfaran bowed his thanks in a circle to all the trees making sure he did not miss one Sprite. He took his hat off with a flourish and waved it around over his head causing the tassels to do their own colorful dance.

Procelina with her acute vision looked at all the trees and could see all the Sprites high up on the limbs each in turn taking his/her hat off and waving it around back at Hotenfaran in acknowledgement. She waved her hands back at them and blew kisses many times around. This caused some of the male Sprites to jump up and down and wave and throw kisses wildly back at Procelina. They had never received air kisses from a fairy. They tried to catch each air kiss so as to keep it as a souvenir for all to see.

"Well, Spindle, does this mean that you too are coming with us on this journey to the Land of Evil and Darkness?" King Gateskin extended his hand to Spindle in welcome and thanks to him for coming so far with his children and enabling them to complete the journey safely with the aid of his fellow Sprites.

"If you will have me, King Gateskin. I would be honored to assist you in any way that I can." As he said this, Spindle took his green hat off his head and bowed to the king. His hat had been almost invisible because it was the same green as his unruly green hair.

Serena found herself laughing again at her friend as she danced around in a circle swinging her dress and cloak back and forth. As Serena did this, she felt a bulge in the pocket of her cloak which caused her to remember she still had the Memory Scroll that her mother had entrusted her to give to her father.

Serena pulled it out of her pocket and looked at it. It was blank as she had expected and it would only become visible in the hands of her father. Serena promptly walked over to hand it to him to not only fulfill her promise to her mother but also because her curiosity was getting the better of her. Serena wondered what her mother had to say to her father but did not want anyone else to know.

King Gateskin took the scroll into his hands and looked down at it with a puzzled expression on his face. He rolled it up quickly and put it away much to the surprise of his children who were waiting to hear what their mother had written to their father.

"Father, aren't you going to tell us what Mother has written to you? Is it a secret that you cannot share with us?" Serena looked very disappointed as she probed further.

"If you cannot tell us, we could always try to guess so you won't get into trouble with Mother." She called Simon and Catalina over so they could triple their powers of thinking and reading minds to try to decipher what their mother had written on the Memory Scroll.

"Serena, dear one, it is not necessary for you to know this just yet. All in due time, my child. I promise to tell you after we complete this task and are safely tucked back home." King

Gateskin waved his hands over his children to calm them all down and prepare them for the dangers they would surely face on the journey ahead.

King Gateskin also conjured up a feast for the eyes and nose and lastly for the mouth to enjoy before they could continue on the trip. They all needed sustenance and strength to take them safely to their destination. They all settled down on the grass under the largest tree to enjoy the feast on a lovely golden cloth which appeared on the grass to hold all the delicacies that appeared soon afterward.

After performing this spell of conjuring up a feast Gateskin thought back to his farm and all the vegetables that he raised and the animals he tended. That was so much more fulfilling than conjuring up food and it all tasted better too fresh from the land. But he shook these thoughts off and got his mind back to the present.

For the time being the Memory Scroll was forgotten by all but King Gateskin. He was a little confused about the message at present but he would keep working it out in his mind until he could figure it out. It must be important to

Solinara or she wouldn't have sent it when she did.

***

It was getting late and too dark to continue. The group was full to bursting from the feast provided by King Gateskin and looked like they needed to sleep it off awhile.

King Gateskin announced, "It is time for everyone to get some much-needed rest before continuing on our way. I will take the first watch, Mitteran will take the second and Hotenfaran would take the next while I rest. Procelina will relieve her husband after that if need be. We will each be allowed two hours of rest to ensure we feel refreshed enough to continue."

Six hours later the group was on their way to the Land of Evil and Darkness to rescue Mitteran's family. The new adventure would soon begin.

A CONJURING OF SPELLS

CHAPTER 43

The plan was to travel together under an Invisible Curtain Spell provided by Procelina once again to keep them safe and out of sight for as long as possible. Once they got to the outskirts of Parotovina, Hotenfaran would walk into the village to ask for assistance. He was to say that he was trying to find his wife who was visiting with friends in the village. She had neglected to give him the address of the people she was staying with but he knew the name of the family – Skolly which was Mitteran's last name.

Once Hotenfaran had the attention of some of the villagers and was engaging them in conversation as to the direction of the Skolly's cottage, Procelina would sneak in under the Invisibility Spell and appear at the Skolly's cottage ahead of her husband. She would prepare Mitteran's wife by putting her in a trance until Hotenfaran could arrive.

Once Hotenfaran arrived there, he was going to explain to Mitteran's wife what he planned to do under a Staglemite spell so as to keep their thoughts safe from the mind of the King and his men.

Hotenfaran had previously pocketed a supply of the Staglemite from the cave in case it could be of further use to them in their travels. Once he was back at his sister's home, he planned to break the material down and make other spells from it and add these new incantations to their Book of Spells. It had already exhibited interesting properties that could be useful in hundreds of different ways. It was exciting to think about, but he had to control his thoughts to deal with the present for now. Once a wizard, always a wizard, he thought to himself.

He and Procelina planned to take Mitteran's wife and children back to the cave and keep them safe until Mitteran and King Gateskin could join them. They would then all journey back to Sovorotskina and freedom.

Now if everything worked out, their plans would come to fruition; but there was always a chance that something could go wrong.

A NEW PLAN IS FINALIZED

CHAPTER 44

Mitteran and King Gateskin had their own agenda to take care of at this point. They planned to enter the village under the guise of shepherds traveling through to find their flock that had wandered away from them. King Gateskin was going to provide their disguises which would be unbreakable until they reached the cave with as many of the Descendants of the TOs as they could find.

Mitteran said, "I will get all the Descendants I know to meet in the square by sending them a message in code that only the Descendants knew how to decipher. This code was the code of their forefathers and only used in emergencies."

In order to get these Descendants of the TOs out of the Land of Darkness and Evil, it would take a very special fairy power or a combination of all the powers of Procelina and the children to change these people into sheep which could in turn be herded out of the village by the shepherds, Mitteran and King Gateskin in disguise.

Spindle had his orders from King Gateskin to get the Sprites around the village of Parotovina to cause as much distraction as they could muster in order to help the shepherds rescue the descendants of the TOs out of the village as quickly as possible.

After Spindle had spoken to the Sprites, they were more than happy to help out. The Sprites had been aware of many atrocities under the rule of King Kaposkaran and would do anything to put a stop to his evil ways. They knew that some of their fellow Sprites had been held captive for years by the King and his wizards. They were unable to free them on their own. They sent their thoughts to these captives to tell them to gather in the square when the distraction began.

Everything was in place and everyone had a job to do and knew just what was expected of him or her. All the rescuers could do now was to follow through with the plan and hope and pray that all their preparations would come to fruition.

THE RESCUE BEGINS

CHAPTER 45

The gate was closed but this did not deter Mitteran and King Gateskin who waved at the Gatekeeper to get his attention as they got closer. Mitteran knew this man so he asked King Gateskin, "I should not speak to the Head Guard. He knows me well and would recognize my voice. You should do it."

King Gateskin assured Mitteran, "Not to worry, Mitteran. This disguise is so convincing that even our voices will not betray our origins or accents."

Just the same, King Gateskin stepped forward to speak with the Gatekeeper. "We are shepherds who have lost our sheep that wandered this way."

As King Gateskin was keeping the Gatekeeper busy Mitteran was sending his thoughts in the Old Code to the Descendants of the TOs telling them, "Go quickly to the square and do not take anything with you but your families. You will be changed into sheep. Do not be alarmed about this prospect for this is the only safe way to get you out of the village under the eyes of the King and his men."

There was much grumbling from them as Mitteran listened to their confused mutterings but soon they all came to a consensus that this was the only way to escape unharmed. They promised to go to their homes as quickly as possible without causing any alarm and bring their families to the square and wait there for further word from Mitteran.

Mitteran told them, "The next thing you will hear from me is a chant, then you will become sheep. Stay close together and do not allow the children to wander away from you. I need you to follow the two shepherds at the gate out of the city as quickly and as quietly as possible."

At the same time outside the Village, Procelina and the children under an Invisible Curtain Spell were working tirelessly combining their powers. They finally came up with a splendid spell that would be forever known as, The Flock of D's (Descendants) Spell. King Gateskin was to send a mind message to Procelina when they were ready for the spell to be cast. It had to be done just at the right moment in order not to cause any alarm from the villagers or the King and his men.

The Gatekeeper looked around and said to the shepherds, "That is strange. I never saw any sheep coming this way. Maybe it was when I was away from my post. I had a problem on the road on my way back here and it took a long time to fix my wagon wheel. Well, it is against my better judgment but I will let you pass. Do it as quickly as you can. I don't want the King to be disturbed during his meal. He is not forgiving about interruptions." The Gatekeeper opened the gate convinced after much discussion with King Gateskin that they were indeed just harmless shepherds looking for their flock. Indeed, you could say they were gathering the lost flock of Ds of the TOs.

They both moved through the village looking around them as if trying to find their flock. They could see a large gathering of the Ds standing around closely together at the square. As King Gateskin alerted Procelina that now was the time for the spell to be cast, she sent the chant to Mitteran who in turn sent it in code to the Ds.

As Mitteran did this, there was a loud ruckus from the trees that bordered the village. The sounds became so annoying the other villagers milling outside their homes rushed into their cottages and closed their doors to keep out the sound.

The only people that were unaffected by this ruckus were the Ds who needed to keep their minds open to the chant that was now coming to them.

Listen to me.
Soon you will see.
I will take you out of this evil place.
On all fours you will walk, not race.
Do not be forlorn
For soon you will be in the land where your
forefathers were born.

Before their very eyes the Ds were transformed into a flock of sheep that at the shepherds' cue began to follow Mitteran and King Gateskin two by two out of the square toward the gate. The Sprites kept up the ruckus until they saw the gate open again and the shepherds safely leading all the sheep out of the village.

King Gateskin went to the back of the flock and used his shepherd's stick to guide the sheep out as quickly as possible toward Mitteran who was now outside the entrance to the village. The sheep were very excited now and began to baa more loudly. King Gateskin sent a message to Mitteran that he needed to send the sheep a code to calm them down.

Mitteran did just that.

Relax my friends.
Now listen to me.
You are almost at the gate's end.
Please be quiet, don't you see?
You will all soon be free.

As soon as the sheep received the coded message, they again became calmer. Once they were all outside the gate the shepherds moved the sheep more quickly along the path toward the cave at the base of Crotesia Mountain where they were to meet the others.

Behind them the village was now back to normal since the Sprites were no longer causing the distraction. The Sprites had watched from high up in the trees to ensure every last one of the sheep were safely outside the border of the Land of Darkness and Evil before bringing the ruckus to a halt.

There was much celebrating by the Sprites, for they had seen the day finally come that the Ds were free to return to their homes. The Sprites were pleased to have played a significant though small part in this memorable rescue.

King Gateskin smiled as he heard the whisperings of the Sprites in celebration. Spindle was up in the trees with his fellow Sprites celebrating.

He would have to make a point to tell Spindle how helpful his fellow Sprites had been in the rescue. King Gateskin would pass on the praise to Abason also once he returned home.

***

At the palace of King Kaposkaran the guards were alarmed by all the noise. They went back inside the palace to tell their King about it. But one guard said, "No, we must not tell the King about this. We don't know what caused it. What would we tell him? He will kill us for disturbing his mid-day meal. You know what happened to the guards in the past who disturbed him unnecessarily. Let's just watch and listen. There is nothing to report now. It is all quiet now. Just a bunch of sheep leaving the village with two shepherds."

What the guards did not know was that Procelina had put a Cloak of Silence Spell over the castle interior so that the King could not hear any of the noise. If the guards had tried to tell the King about it, he wouldn't have believed them.

Procelina was also responsible for keeping the guards busy holding their ears and closing their eyes during the gathering of the flock of Ds. So, they never saw the Ds gathering and turning into sheep. They only saw them leaving the village.

CHAPTER 46

Procelina had sent the children back to the cave for their safekeeping and to wait for their father and the sheep or Ds of the TOs. They were very powerful for children and had worked tirelessly with Procelina to put together the Invisibility Spell for her and Hotenfaran to use in order to get into the Village of Parotovina.

As Procelina and Hotenfaran were on their way to the gate of the Village of Parotovina under the Invisibility Spell, Hotenfaran noticed that the Gatekeeper was the same man who he had helped with a broken wheel. He told Procelina to go on ahead and he would follow shortly. She scurried away in the guise of a mouse. Hotenfaran had plans of his own now that he knew the Gatekeeper.

The Gatekeeper looked up with a look of pleasant surprise as Hotenfaran suddenly appeared out of nowhere at the gate. "Well, my friend, what brings you to the Village of Parotovina?" the Gatekeeper inquired.

"Well, this is a surprise to see you too. I didn't realize you were the Gatekeeper of Parotovina. This is quite an important position."

"Well, it's a job like any other but it does come with more responsibility to the King. You were very kind to help me recently with my wheel. I don't know what King Kaposkaran would have done if I couldn't get back here to my post. He had sent me on an errand. The King was upset with me for being late. I thank you again, my friend. What can I do for you?"

"No need to thank me again. It was a pleasure to help you. I am sure you would have done the same for me. Well, there is something. I have a little problem that I hope you can help me with. I need first to find my wife who is visiting with

Mrs. Skolly and get her out of Parotovina safely without alarming the King's guards. Do you think you can make sure that I am not stopped from going to find my wife and then leaving unannounced?"

"I will do what I can but you must leave by the back of the woods and as quickly as possible. The guards are on the lookout but I will try to get them to move away from the Skolly's house so you can leave without harm."

"Thank you, kind sir. Let me introduce myself. I am Hotenfaran. What is your name?"

"I am known as Kelleran. It is a pleasure to meet you, Hotenfaran, and to finally pay back your kindness. I think I understand why you do not want the guards to see you. You are a wizard, are you not? I do not need to know what you are up to for I know the King would arrest you and have you hung for coming into his village. I don't agree with how the King rules Parotovina. I do not want to know your business so I will turn my back on whatever you do. Now you must hurry along. Good luck, my friend."

"It is my pleasure to meet you, Kelleran. I am sorry I cannot tell you what my business is but I assure you what I do will be for the common good. I thank you so much for your assistance."

Procelina exhaled a deep sigh of relief as she received the message from King Gateskin that they were safely out of the village and on their way to the cave. She had now reached Mitteran's house after changing back into a fairy. She knocked softly at the door. Mrs. Skolly came to the door and asked in a puzzled manner, "Yes, can I help you, madame?"

"Yes, my name is Procelina. I am a friend of your husband's. Please, may I come in? Mitteran sent me here to take you and your children away from the village to meet him. My husband is coming very shortly to assist me in getting you all away safely."

"Okay, please come in but I don't understand, Procelina. Why? Are we in danger? This is our home. My husband is expected back soon. He promised me he would return and then we would leave together," Mrs. Skolly spoke softly as she looked around. She was frightened that her children would be alarmed if they saw their mother so disturbed.

"There is a lot to tell you but there is no time now. We must leave as soon as my husband, Hotenfaran, arrives. I promise you we will keep you and your children safe so you can be with your husband. I am sorry we could not prepare you more for what is ahead. You just have to trust me."

Procelina was sitting and talking to Mrs. Skolly trying to calm her down with a spell and explain that she was there to help. Procelina was ever vigilant, listening and watching for any danger around them as Hotenfaran came to the door and slipped in quietly. Hotenfaran explained to Mitteran's wife what was happening out in the village. Mrs. Skolly and her children had become frightened when they first heard the ruckus a short time ago.

"Everything will be fine but we must hurry for your safety and that of your children. Please believe us that we are here by your husband's request. He could not be here to get you himself. But you will see him shortly. Please gather a few things that you may need and have your children do the same. We must travel as light as possible."

Hotenfaran had not quite convinced Mrs. Skolly that all would be fine if they would just follow him and Procelina out through the back door and through the woods to the mountain so they could be reunited with Mitteran.

Mrs. Skolly still insisted, "I will not go without my husband's confirmation. I don't know who you are and can't trust you without receiving a message from my husband confirming this trip."

Hotenfaran just shook his head at the stubbornness of this woman. But of course, he knew what it was like to have a stubborn wife; Procelina was the queen of stubborn.

Procelina gave Hotenfaran her steely-eyed gaze when she read his thoughts about her stubbornness. Procelina waved her hand at Hotenfaran and responded that she loved him no matter what he said about her.

Hotenfaran winked at Procelina then proceeded to send a mind code to Mitteran about his reticent wife. Messages were received quickly back and forth under the protection of the Staglemite now that Hotenfaran has figured out how to open the channels one way only to decipher the messages clearly for his own ears.

Mitteran's message to his wife was something that only they knew about each other. Once Mitteran's message was received by his wife, she became very docile and hastily gathered her children and a few belongings and followed Hotenfaran and Procelina under the curtain of the Invisibility Spell out the back door of the cottage. Once outside the boundaries of the village they quickened their pace to reach the path leading to Crotesia Mountain.

DANGER LURKING

CHAPTER 47

"What are we going to do? We cannot go back to the village for we will surely be killed and our families too! We shouldn't have run away. It wasn't anything to be afraid of – it was just a loud noise, wasn't it?" The four guards looked at one another for an answer to their dilemma.

They had been the ones responsible for guarding the mouth and back of the cave for the Head Guard, Mitteran. They had run a few miles back into the woods away from the cave and now were lost.

They had to come up with a reason for their lateness in getting back to the village. Surely Mitteran had brought back the prisoner and some of the rescuers to King Kaposkaran by now. All they had to do was go back to the village and tell the King they were protecting Mitteran's back from anyone coming up behind him.

One guard who had been tormented by the Sprites finally spoke up. "I don't think he will believe us. We must find some villagers to bring back with us as a peace offering." The guard put his finger to his lips and looked at his fellow guards as the sound of pounding feet could be heard in the distance.

They followed the sounds until they reached a break in the trees and could peek through the trees and brush to see what was passing by on the path heading away from Parotovina. They could not believe their eyes when they saw a large flock of sheep walking two by two led by a tall shepherd at the front and another very large shepherd at the back of the flock. It took several minutes before the flock finally passed by. The guards watched and wondered where they were going.

The curious guards decided they would follow the flock to see where they were going and maybe they could capture a few sheep along with the shepherds and bring them back to the King as an offering.

Unbeknownst to the guards, they were also being watched. The Sprites, ever vigilant, were listening in on the guards' conversation and knew what they were up to. The Sprites spread the word to the other Sprites further up the path to keep a look out for the guards and try to hamper their progress and prevent them from going after the shepherds and the flock of sheep.

It was imperative the Ds got to the cave safely without harm. The Sprites had promised King Gateskin they would keep careful watch over the forest and the path and be the King's eyes and ears. They always kept their promises for they were honorable creatures.

The rumblings started again. The Sprites were banging the trees with sticks at intervals timed so as to be the most effective in sound and vibration to the humans' ears.

The guards stopped and looked around them. It could not be happening again. The sound was getting louder and louder. The four guards put their hands over their ears and were yelling back and forth to each other just to be heard. "It's happening again. What do we do?"

Each was afraid to run and be called a coward once again. But what other choice did they have. The sound was getting painful to their ears as they each took a step forward.

One guard, at the back of group, decided to turn around and go back to the forest. As he took one step back at a time, he noticed the sound decreased in his ears so that he no longer had pain. He called ahead to the other guards, "Turn around and walk back to me. If you do that the pain will subside."

They looked at him puzzled at his request, but they did what he said because they couldn't stand the pain in their heads and ears that the noise was causing them. They soon realized that their pain decreased too with each step back they took.

They exchanged looks and agreed. "We can not go forward. We must return to the village and tell the King of what we saw and experienced. King Kaposkaran would surely believe us and send more men to help us capture the sheep and bring them back to the village for him."

The Sprites had again succeeded in deterring the progress of the guards from following and possibly capturing the Ds and bringing them back to the village. The Sprites knew that the guards could come back with reinforcements but the Sprites would keep a close watch and pass the word to the other Sprites that lived in the trees surrounding the Land of Darkness and Evil of what the guards were planning to do once they got back to the village.

The Sprites hadn't noticed that one of the guards was still at the cave. He had fallen asleep and hadn't heard anything going on. He was a little hard of hearing to begin with and could sleep through a tornado.

The guard woke up suddenly when he realized he was alone. He looked around and whispered, "Where is everyone?"

He was known to be the eyes and ears of the King. But what he didn't mention to the King was that he couldn't hear well. If the King knew this fact he would have been strung up in the square. He did not have a family so he didn't have anyone else to worry about but himself. He felt free to be away from the village and King Kaposkaran and his evil ways. He promised the King that he would keep him abreast of what was happening. Right now, he had no idea about that.

He crept into the cave to hide out until he could come up with something else to do. He couldn't just go back to the village if he didn't have a good reason. He would wait awhile and see if any of the other guards showed up.

The guard found a spot to hide in and after getting comfortable he promptly fell asleep once again. Gateskin's three children were in the cave unbeknownst to the guard.

Catalina had wandered away from her siblings and was looking around for some special rocks with rainbow sparkles in them, known as Rainbow Rocks. These rocks were known to be magical if they were used by a person who knew how to caste a spell.

She was so busy gathering these rocks that she stumbled upon the guard who abruptly woke up and stared at her. She screeched loud enough to warn Serena and Simon who came running.

Serena came to her sister's aid first. She saw the guard and pulled her sister away from him, safely putting Catalina behind herself. Simon was beside Serena a second later and stared at the guard protectively holding onto Catalina who was still shaking from the shock of seeing the guard.

"Who are you? What are you doing here?" Serena queried in a strong voice meant to intimidate the man.

"I'm sorry. Can you please speak up? I don't hear too well."

"I said, who are you and what are you doing here?"

"I...I...fell asleep and my fellow guards are all gone. I don't know where they went. Who are you?"

Serena stepped closer to the man and said, "We are the children of King Gateskin. You better leave before he gets here. He wouldn't take too kindly to you scaring his children."

"Oh no. I didn't mean to scare you. I fell asleep here. I was going to leave as soon as I thought of an excuse why I was separated from the other guards. I don't know what happened. I slept quite soundly and didn't hear a thing. Please explain that to your father. I mean no harm to you."

The children looked at the guard who was quite distraught and frightened at the prospect of meeting their father and explaining his plight.

In the meantime, the guard secretly sent a message with his powers of messaging to the King and waited. He wanted to try to capture these children and bring them back to the King.

He would be greatly rewarded for securing King Gateskin's three children. He would do what he could to turn them to the ways of the evil King. He knew he may even be given a place at the Palace to live. He smiled as he envisioned all this happening.

AN UNEXPECTED FIND

CHAPTER 48

"There is the cave up ahead, King Gateskin. I will bring the sheep around to the back and corral them there. I do have some powers of my own to use which I have been hiding from my men and the King for years. I might be a little rusty but I think I can conjure up a fence to corral the sheep for the time being until Procelina arrives to change them back to the

Ds." Mitteran waved at King Gateskin as he led the sheep around to the back of the cave.

King Gateskin acknowledged Mitteran with a wave before he disappeared into the cave to check on the children. He whistled a special song that only his children would recognize. They soon jumped out at him from the shadows and enveloped him in hugs and kisses, even Simon hugged his father tightly instead of just shaking his hand.

Serena stepped forward after greeting her father and announced, "We found a guard sleeping in the cave."

"Where is he?" Gateskin asked in a shocked voice. "Are you all okay? Did he harm any of you?"

"No, Father. We are fine. He didn't try to hurt us. Maybe I should let him explain."

Catalina stepped forward to add, "Father, I was the one to find him. He was sleeping and I was searching for some Rainbow Rocks and there he was."

"Thank you, Catalina. Now you must stay back while I go talk to him. Okay? Go with your brother and sister now."

Catalina nodded solemnly and walked out of the cave with Serena and Simon.

Once King Gateskin was assured that the children were all safe, he walked deeper into the cave and saw the man inside the same cage where he had been kept previously by Mitteran.

The man hung his head and did not look up at him until Gateskin called out to him. "Who are you, sir?"

"Oh, King Gateskin, the kind King. It is a pleasure to meet you. I have heard so much about you from my fellow guards. They are fearful of you. They know how strong you are." The guard's voice shook as he avoided meeting Gateskin's steely gaze.

"What is your name, sir?" Gateskin ignored what the guard said to try to make him let his defenses down.

"I...I am Botular. I am the eyes and ears of King Kaposkaran. He gave me this auspicious position to keep eyes and ears on the Head Guard, Mitteran. I don't think the King trusts him. Evidently he has reason to since you have escaped from Mitteran."

"Why are you still here then? Evidently you didn't do your job. I wonder what the King would say about that."

"Oh please, kind king. I cannot go back there. He will surely string me up in the square."

"Did you hear anything that was said here by Mitteran?"

"No, King Gateskin. I must explain. I am hard of hearing and have been since I was just a child. My uncle used to beat me about the head and injured my ears. He sold me to the King when I was just a boy. I never told the King that I couldn't hear well. He would have killed me right then and my uncle would have been hung. Even though I did not like my uncle he was the only father I knew. The King killed my parents when I was just a baby because they had powers but refused to use them for him," the guard explained and covered his face with his hands.

"I am sorry for you, Botular. What are you going to do now?"

"I don't know, King Gateskin. I am fearful King Kaposkaran will realize that I haven't returned or kept him abreast of what is going on. Of course, I don't know anything at this point. I have nothing to tell him. What should I do?"

The guard neglected to tell King Gateskin that he sent a message to his king that he would turn the children to his side and deliver them to the palace.

King Gateskin opened the door of the cage in the cave and let the guard out. "It is up to you what you want to do. You can either go back to your village or stay with us and be our eyes and ears against your king."

"Yes, I can do that, King Gateskin. I will do that for you as long as I don't ever have to go back to Parotovina," the guard begged Gateskin with pleading eyes as he bowed in front of him. He realized this was his only alternative since he never received word back from his king.

"Well, if you promise to stay true to us and never harm anyone in my party."

"Of course, I promise to be your eyes and ears, most gracious king. I want to live in your village, if you will accept me. I may not have good hearing but I have some of my parents' powers that aid me in doing my job."

Gateskin looked at Botular but was hesitant to believe him.

"What are these powers you have, Botular?" Gateskin looked kindly but hesitantly on the guard who was shivering and still frightened.

"I can hide away and blend into my surroundings. That way I can sneak up on others and listen more closely since I can't hear unless I am closer. I am also able to send messages to the King through his wizards by my mind. That is the only way I could do my job for the King. He never knew I had powers of my own. I was afraid to tell him."

"I see. So, if I ask you to get closer to the guards, you can tell me what they are going to do?"

"Well, yes, I could if I knew where they were. They left without me. I had blended into my surroundings. They evidently didn't notice I was missing. When they get back to the village, they will tell the King that I was missing."

"Okay, Botular, come with me. I have a job for you to do."

Botular jumped up and followed King Gateskin out of the cave.

When they left the cave Gateskin took Botular to the edge of trees surrounding Mt. Crotesia and told him to stay there to keep watch for any guards who might return looking for him.

"Okay, I promise I will alert you if they come back, my King. Can I call you, my King?"

"Soon you may as long as you prove yourself worthy of being a citizen of Sorovotskina."

"Yes, I will. I will prove myself to you, King Gateskin. I will."

Gateskin watched Botular as he settled down next to a tree and blended into the tree trunk in front of his eyes. The King walked away and set off through the forest to look for Procelina and Hotenfaran. He came upon Spindle who was whispering to the other Sprites giving them the latest news to relay to his father and Serena's mother.

King Gateskin extended his hand in greeting to Spindle and carefully shook the little Sprite boy's hand so as not to injure him. He said, "Spindle, I can't thank you and all the other Sprites enough for all that you and they have done for us. They certainly are a noisy bunch of little creatures but their noise is sweet music to my ears. They have saved our hides a few times already. I plan on thanking your father in person as soon as we get back too. He should be very proud of you. You are a brave and courageous young Sprite." King Gateskin noticed that Spindle's face had become quite flushed and he was tongue tied. He evidently wasn't comfortable receiving compliments.

"I....I...well, um...I don't know what to say, King Gateskin. I am honored by your kind words. Thank you! I know I speak for all the Sprites when I say that it is a pleasure to serve you." Spindle removed his hat and bowed as deeply as he could without hitting his head on the ground. A cheering could be heard from the Sprites nearby enthusiastically supporting Spindle's words.

King Gateskin waved to them in acknowledgement and thanks before he picked up Spindle (much to his surprise and delight) and put the boy Sprite on his shoulder as he continued walking through the forest to look for Procelina and Hotenfaran.

While King Gateskin had been conversing with Spindle he had forgotten some of the anxiety he had been feeling over the lateness of the arrival of Mitteran's family escorted by Procelina and Hotenfaran. King Gateskin trusted his brother-in-law and his wife and knew that if they were late it had to be something serious but King Gateskin was sure Hotenfaran and Procelina could handle anything that came their way.

King Gateskin trudged deeper into the forest with Spindle bouncing along on his shoulder holding on for dear life to the collar of King

Gateskin's shirt. He whispered to Spindle, "I'm a little worried about Hotenfaran and Procelina. They are very late. That is not like them at all. Do you think you can maybe ask the Sprites if they know something about the group's whereabouts?"

Spindle sent a message to the nearest Sprite who in turn sent the message along to each tree Sprite to see if they had seen the wizard and fairy anywhere in the forest.

The messages came back swiftly. Spindle related, "They have been spotted a mile and a half away in the forest. They stopped so that the family they were escorting could rest. The Sprites promised they would keep many eyes on the group to make sure they would make their way safely to you, King Gateskin."

King Gateskin said, "Thank you, my dear little friends, for indulging me once again. I guess all I can do is sit and wait right here for the group to arrive." He didn't want to scare the group by coming up on them unexpectedly. They would most probably be undercover of Procelina's Invisible Curtain Spell. He could very well bump into them without seeing them.

King Gateskin concentrated on sending his thoughts to Hotenfaran that he was waiting for him in the forest near the cave. To allay his fears King Gateskin requested that Hotenfaran respond in code if there was anything wrong.

Hotenfaran received his brother-in-law's message and responded back in kind, "Everything is indeed on schedule without any problems." Hotenfaran promised. "We will see you shortly. Don't be surprised if we come upon you and pop out of the Invisible Curtan Spell."

No sooner did King Gateskin receive this message that another important message was sent his way, this one from Mitteran. He urgently requested, "Please come immediately to the field next to the cave. There is something you must see for yourself."

King Gateskin told Spindle, as he lifted him off his shoulder to the ground, "Spindle, I must leave you in charge of escorting the group, when they arrive, back to the cave. I need to go back to the cave to assist Mitteran right away. Tell the group I would meet them all there shortly. Can you do that for me, my little man?

I have full confidence you will do a great job as always."

Spindle was at first speechless, which is something for a Sprite. They never seem to run out of things to say. They even talk to rocks.

He finally replied, "Um, yes, I will do my best to follow your orders, King Gateskin. Thank you, sir, for entrusting this very important assignment to such an unworthy Sprite." Spindle bowed low to show his reverence to the King.

"Oh Spindle, you are quite a character! You are very worthy of this and other assignments. I feel that you will be one of my most trusted soldiers when we get back to Sovorotskina. I will need to find you an important position in the ranks of my guards."

"Oh, my goodness! Thank you! Thank you so much, my King. I will make you proud of me and do my very best to honor you," Spindle said as he stood up and squared his shoulders while his face flushed with pride.

"My dear young Sprite, you have more than shown me how worthy you are. At your post now, Spindle. See you at the cave shortly."

King Gateskin rushed out of the forest to the back of the cave where Mitteran was standing at the newly made corral that he had conjured up to keep the sheep together. He wore a proud look on his face at his accomplishments. The corral looked a little lopsided but sturdy enough to keep the flock in place temporarily.

Nothing else seemed to be out of place as King Gateskin walked over to stand next to Mitteran. King Gateskin was about to ask Mitteran what was so urgent that requested his presence when he noticed one of the sheep stood out above the rest. It was completely black all over and had long pointed horns that stood up over the heads of the rest of the sheep. King Gateskin was puzzled too. He had never seen anything like this creature. He wondered how they had not noticed him before they had gotten to the cave.

AN INTERESTING DISCOVERY

CHAPTER 49

"So, King Gateskin, what do you think it is? Do you think it could be a real animal that got mixed in with the sheep on the way here?" Mitteran looked extremely befuddled over this strange discovery.

"I really don't know what it could be. I am as much at odds about it as you are. I am not getting any messages from its mind either. It seems to be able to block me out. Hmmm…very interesting indeed!"

"What's wrong, King Gateskin, is it sending you a message? For God's sake man, tell me what it is saying to you?" Mitteran voice was betraying his impatience due to extreme anxiety over his concern for his family.

"Oh, never mind, I don't have time for this nonsense. Where is my family? Did you not say they should have been here by now? What could have happened to them? I was so involved with building this corral and then discovering this creature, I did not realize how much time had passed. I will go out into the forest myself and bring them back here." Mitteran was heading away from the corral when King Gateskin stopped him with the power of his mind.

King Gateskin sent a much-needed message about Mitteran's family to allay Mitteran's fears and anxiety, "Do not fear. Your family is safe and, on their way here now as we speak." Gateskin admonished himself. "This was something I should have done much sooner than this." But King Gateskin was so busy

346

studying the strange creature himself that he had lost track of time too.

"Thank you, King Gateskin. I am sorry for doubting you and your brother-in-law but I won't be completely relieved until I can hold them in my arms and see for myself that they are unharmed." Mitteran bowed to King Gateskin and quickly hurried to the forest path to meet his family.

***

Unknownst to Mitteran and King Gateskin, there was trouble brewing for Mitteran's family.

Procelina held up her hand to stop the group from moving forward. She exchanged messages with Hotenfaran about a possible scouting party looking for them ahead.

He nodded and put an invisibility cloak over the Head Guard's family as he stepped outside of it to investigate. Procelina tried to grab his cloak to keep him from doing this but missed by inches.

She sent her thoughts to Hotenfaran about his safety. "You mustn't do this, Hotenfaran. There are too many of them. You cannot stop them. Please come back inside the Cloak Spell."

Back in the Cave of Crotesia, the three children sensed there was something wrong. They felt the air around them in the distance and knew someone was out there.

Serena sent her thoughts to her aunt and uncle who they knew were on their way there. "You must be careful. There are some people coming your way. I can't tell if they are Parotovinans or not. Do you need help from us?"

"Thank you, dear niece. I am trying to get your uncle back under the Invisibility Cloak that he created. But you know how stubborn he is. He thinks he can take care of the scouting party himself. I think they were sent by the King to capture us and Mitteran's family."

Simon was listening in on his sister's conversation with their aunt and interrupted unexpectedly. "Sorry to jump in on your thoughts but I know what to do. I can fly over the area and distract them with the help of you and Uncle Hotenfaran."

"Wait a minute," Catalina announced. "I can help too. I can use the spell to change the men into animals. I really like pigs, don't you? Can I please do this?" she begged sweetly.

"Oh, my goodness. You children have such innovative minds. I think that would be lovely, Simon. Your suggestion to change them into pigs is excellent, Catalina. Let's do this," Procelina giggled. She sent these messages to Hotenfaran who came back to the safety of the Cloak Spell.

"I agree, Procelina. There are too many of them. I don't want our nieces and nephew in danger even though I do like their ideas."

Serena declared, "We will be fine, Uncle Hotenfaran. I will watch over them and assist them with the spell. We can do this long distance like we did with the sheep."

Procelina agreed and added, "Send me your thoughts and I will help you by sending the spell directly to the men."

Serena helped her brother and sister get the spell just right before sending it along to their aunt. They waited holding their breaths as Procelina thanked them and proceeded to perform the spell.

"Do you think it worked, Serena?" Catalina asked excitedly as she jumped up and down too nervous to keep still.

"We will know soon. We may even feel it."

Simon asked, "Why don't I fly over them to see if it worked?"

Before Serena could answer him, she got a message from Procelina.

A HAPPY REUNION

CHAPTER 50

Spindle had been daydreaming when he finally heard a shuffling of several feet along the path and looked up to see a cloud of dust kicked up a few feet in front of him. Coming out of the dusty cloud he spotted first Hotenfaran, then Procelina leading a woman, a boy and girl toward him.

Spindle ran ahead to greet them, "Hi, I'm Spindle. I was entrusted by the King to escort you back to the cave."

The children giggled at Spindle and said in amazement, "He's a Sprite! Wow, we never saw a Sprite up close. Hi Spindle. Nice to meet you!"

Spindle bowed to the children and shook their larger hands gently so as not to injure his own. As they were heading toward the cave, Mitteran ran toward them nearly knocking over Spindle in his haste to get to his family.

The Sprite luckily saw him coming and just in time flew up into the nearest tree to let him pass. He knew what it was like to miss your family. Spindle certainly missed his parents but he would see them in due time after he completed his final task.

"Daddy, we found you! We thought you were never coming back to us!" His six-year-old daughter, Tessa, exclaimed as she tightly hugged his knees and would not let go.

Mitteran's son, Allonso, or Al, as he wanted to be called now that he was thirteen, grasped his father in an unexpected bear hug. He had stopped hugging his father over the past year or so considering himself too old to hug or kiss his parents anymore. Evidently this was a special occasion for he was now hugging his father very tightly. Mitteran returned their hugs and added a few kisses before Al backed away.

Mrs. Skolly was standing aside to allow her husband time with their children. She said, "The children have been very frightened and did not think they would ever see you again. But thanks to the quick thinking and powers of both the Wizard Hotenfaran, and the Fairy Procelina, we are all now reunited."

"Yes, thank God, my dear!" Mitteran pulled his wife in a tight embrace and kissed her several times all over her face for the sheer joy of seeing her. Mitteran desperately loved his family and thanks to the help of King Gateskin, Hotenfaran and Procelina he would now be able to begin a new life away from the Land of Darkness and Evil.

Now that they were safe, Mrs. Skolly felt she needed to apologize to the Fairy Procelina, and the Wizard Hotenfaran for not trusting them at first.

She turned toward them and said, "I am sorry for not trusting you. I am so very grateful for what you have done for my children and me. I don't know how to thank you. I'm afraid I was rude to you both too. I never gave you my first name either. It is Leanna."

"It's a pleasure to call you by your surname, Leanna. Please do not thank us. We wanted to help Mitteran. You are family to us since you are fellow Sovorotskinans," Hotenfaran and Procelina said in unison with a slight bow.

"Oh, Mitteran, you told them?" Leanna gasped as she looked at her husband, surprised and a little apprehensive at the same time.

"It is all right, my dear. They are our family now. We are going to be able to live free and be safe away from King Kaposkaran. He cannot harm us now."

King Gateskin came through the woods and listened and waited until Mitteran finished explaining what their situation would now be before he spoke.

"Leanna, Mitteran is correct. We are your family and we can protect you. You will live in the Village of Sovorotskina where we make our home. I will personally help you get settled when we arrive there."

Leanna and Mitteran looked relieved and happy to have found such a wonderful extended family of friends. Now they would feel safe and their children would grow up without fear under the kind and benevolent ruler, King Gateskin.

Tessa pulled on her father's pants to get his attention. "Daddy, something funny happened when we were walking here."

Mitteran looked down at his daughter and asked, "What happened, sweetheart?"

Leanna picked Tessa up so she could whisper to her father about what had happened on their way.

Her father laughed out loud at what she had told him. "Really? There were a bunch of pigs in the road? I wonder how they got there." He looked over at Procelina and Hotenfaran and they just shrugged their shoulders and smiled. Hotenfaran winked at Mitteran and slapped him on the back as he walked by.

Gateskin chuckled and said, "Now I'm going back to check on our sheep. Take your time with your wife and children, Mitteran. Procelina and Hotenfaran, please come with me. We have some sheep to change back to Ds. I am sure they are getting restless."

A PLEASANT SURPRISE

CHAPTER 51

Gateskin, Procelina and Hotenfaran were observing the strange black animal that had suddenly appeared as Mitteran was building the corral, when the creature's appearance again changed drastically.

With all his powers and keen sense of all things around him King Gateskin never expected to see what was now in front of him. He found that he had actually jumped back a couple of feet from surprise at the transformation.

Standing in the middle of the pen with the sheep was a little boy around the age of five. He did not seem frightened or surprised by his transformation as he looked over at King Gateskin. In fact, he smiled very sweetly at King Gateskin and waved his hand in greeting at Procelina and Hotenfaran as he walked over, between the sheep, to meet the King.

King Gateskin reached over the fence and lifted the boy up and over the rails and wrapped his cloak around the naked boy's body. The boy spoke first. He said in a very soft and sweet voice only a boy of this age has, "I am sorry if I surprised you, King Gateskin. But I did not like being a sheep. You know they are very smelly creatures and it is so hot with all that hair on them. I don't particularly like to eat grass either."

Procelina felt like she was holding her breath as she looked adoringly at the sweet, little angelic boy. Hotenfaran was amazed at what he just witnessed too and wondered how such a young child could perform such magic. He was in awe and planned to find out more.

King Gateskin couldn't help laughing out loud so heartily at the child's words. Upon hearing their father's laughter, the children came rushing out of the cave where they were playing to see what was so funny. Mitteran and his family also heard his hearty laugh and came running through the woods to the path around the back of the cave with Spindle bringing up the rear.

When they all arrived, they just stood looking at the little boy standing in front of King Gateskin. The boy was almost invisible, completely enveloped by the King's large cloak.

King Gateskin looked over at the group that was staring at the little boy and felt he must explain what he had just witnessed. But he must first find out who this young boy was and how he had performed such a difficult transformation spell. He was sure that Hotenfaran would want to know also since he had perfected this very spell in his Book of Spells many years ago.

"My little man, can you please tell us how you managed to transform yourself first into a black horned sheep then into a little boy? This is very powerful magic indeed." Gateksin held his own chin in his hand as he pondered what the boy would give as the answer to his question.

Before he could answer King Gateskin's question, Procelina stepped closer to the boy and looking kindly at him asked, "Are you hungry or cold? I can conjure up some clothes for you along with your favorite foods."

Instantly, Gateskin found his cloak back on his back as she said this.

The boy nodded his head to Procelina. Before he could blink his eyes, she had him outfitted with his own fancy cloak and pointed hat similar to Hotenfaran's. Procelina set a plate with all kinds of foods in front of the boy on a table that suddenly appeared so he could eat to his heart's content.

The boy ate his fill before looking up at them again. He wiped his full mouth and took a long gulp of water then swallowed before speaking, "My name is Arubane. I lived in the village of

Parotovina known as the Land of Darkness and Evil. My parents were a wizard and a fairy that were killed by King Kaposkaran for not doing his evil bidding. Before they were taken away by the King's men, they hid me in the barn with the animals and told me to change myself into a sheep so as not to be seen. They taught me many spells as soon as I was able to walk and talk and understand.

They told me they would come back for me but they never did so I know they are both dead. I lived as a part of the flock in the barn and only changed back to a boy when I needed to eat since I do not like to eat grass or grain."

Arubane continued, "One day I was wandering around as a sheep and noticed the large gathering in the square and watched as they suddenly transformed into sheep. I knew there was a powerful wizard around who must have performed this spell. I saw my chance of getting out of the village if I joined the flock and followed the wizards out of the village; and here I am."

"Thank you, Miss Fairy, for the handsome clothes and delicious food you conjured up for me. Can I stay with you now that I am free of the evil King Kaposkaran?" He turned his little face toward Procelina and showed her his beautiful blue eyes and his most magnificent smile. This gesture softened Procelina's heart and brought tears to her luminous eyes as she looked in turn at Hotenfaran for an answer.

"Well, Hotenfaran, what do you say to this fine little boy? Can he stay with us?" Procelina and the little boy both looked intently at Hotenfaran while he pondered this tough question. Hotenfaran knew that he better think this through carefully or he would hurt Procelina if he gave the wrong answer.

"I think...well...I think it would be a good idea if this fine young man comes back with us to Sovorotskina so we can make a final decision on where he will live. After all, Procelina, we are not sure where we are going to be living yet. But I would be honored to have you with us, little man. Arubane, is it?" Hotenfaran kneeled down to look at the boy more closely. The wizard noticed the deep blue of the boy's eyes were surprisingly like his wife's eyes. This fact startled him to his core.

"Thank you, kind sir, for your invitation. I would be honored to accompany you to your village. I have heard from the Sovorotskinans and my parents of the great Land of Goodness and Light. I would be happy to see it for myself. Is it really beautiful there? Is everything green and plentiful?" Arubane could not curtail his excitement over going to the Sovorotskina with his new friends as he looked expectantly at Hotenfaran for any more news at all of this wonderful Land of Light.

Hotenfaran tried in vain to interrupt the diatribe of this young boy but couldn't get a word in edgewise. Arubane continued with his unending questions.

"Do you have curfews or are your children allowed to go outside and play each day? In Parotovina all the children must be in their homes from noon to sun up. We can only go out to play for a few hours a day and always under the watchful eyes of the King's guards who wander the streets all day and night. If any child is caught outside after noon time without the escort of their parents, the children are taken away to the King's dungeon. Some of my friends were taken there and were never seen again." Arubane's blue eyes grew brighter with each of his surprising statements to the group. He just couldn't seem to get all the information out fast enough.

"There is nothing like that in the Land of Goodness and Light, Arubane. I assure you," Hotenfaran said to the purely evident delight on Arubane's little face.

Procelina enveloped her husband in a tight squeeze to show him how happy she was at his decision to bring the sweet boy, Arubane, back with them to Sovorotskina. Procelina was confident that once they got back there, she could convince Hotenfaran to agree to adopt this darling little parentless and homeless little boy as their son. Procelina could not contain her joy at the prospect of finally being a mother.

She took the boy in her arms to give him a hug to make him feel a part of their group. When Procelina tried to release Arubane from her hug, he held onto her fiercely with his little arms wrapped around her neck. The fairy, for once, was at a loss for words and her eyes prickled from tears that were threatening to fall again. She looked up at her husband as Hotenfaran smiled kindly and lovingly back at her. Sharing her thoughts with Hotenfaran was calming to Procelina since she was concerned about what would happen if things didn't work out and Arubane did not want to be adopted by them.

No sooner were the thoughts of Hotenfaran and Procelina transferred between them than the thoughts of the little boy, Arubane's, much to their surprise and delight, entered both the Wizard's and Fairy's minds.

Arubane had announced by mind transfer. "I would love to be adopted by you and would also love to call you Mother and Father."

Procelina grasped Arubane's and Hotenfaran's hands at the same time and the three of them jumped up and down and spun in a circle of happiness at Arubane's exclamation of acceptance. Procelina and Hotenfaran were to become parents at long last! There would be much rejoicing when the adoption was final.

Hotenfaran looked forward to sending this exciting news to his sister, Queen Solinara, with Procelina's permission of course. Hotenfaran knew how Procelina always liked to be the bearer of good news. Procelina decided that they could both send the announcement at the same time to Queen Solinara. Hearing this Arubane said, "I would also like to send a greeting to my new Aunt Queen Solinara that I am anxious to meet her."

Procelina couldn't help but laugh at her soon-to-be son at his thoughtfulness and sweet nature. She couldn't remember a time when she was happier than right now. Hotenfaran sent the same thought to Procelina.

The three, who would soon be a family, sent their ecstatic news to Queen Solinara, "We are going to be a family! We have a son, Arubane, who you will meet shortly!"

Loud baaing could be heard coming from the corral bringing the threesome out of their happy reverie. Evidently the Ds, who were no longer happy being sheep, were now letting the group know their discomfort loud and clear.

King Gateskin stepped forward to congratulate his soon-to-be nephew, Arubane, that he had found a new home with loving parents. King Gateskin also shook his brother-in-law's hand

and hugged his sister-in-law and wished them all good luck in their wondrous new venture being parents. King Gateskin said, "As soon as we get back home, I will draw up the adoption papers making Arubane legally the son of you both."

"Thank you, dear King Gateskin. We are truly grateful to you." Hotenfaran bowed down to his brother-in-law in thanks.

"Well, what do you say, Procelina and my son, Arubane, shall we work together to transform these poor sheep back into Ds before they lose their voices altogether? Besides, all this baaing is getting on my nerves." Hotenfaran exchanged broad smiles with his wife and newfound son and then began to conjure up the Transformation Spell that Arubane had used on himself earlier.

Before long all the sheep were Ds once again fully clothed with the aid of Procelina and seen stretching and arching their aching backs from being on all fours for so long. The Ds seemed to be relieved that they were now safely out of the Land of Darkness and Evil. Each man looked around for his wife as their wives looked around for their children. Once all families were reunited, they seemed content and wanted to thank their rescuers for the daring and clever rescue of them all.

Many hands were shook, hugs were exchanged and backs were slapped in thanks. But mostly everyone was happy to be away from the evil King Kaposkaran's grip. The next step was for the Ds to decide which village they wanted to go to live. Many of them no longer had any relatives to visit who would know them. The Ds had never been to the villages of their relatives.

Procelina produced a few tables laden with all kinds of food for the Ds to refresh them. After everyone was full to bursting, they expressed their thanks once again.

King Gateskin looked kindly out at the multitude of anxious but relieved faces of the Ds. He extended his hands out to them in greeting and said, "My fellow brothers and sisters, please feel free to follow us back to the Land of Goodness and Light, the Village of Sovorotskina. You are all welcome there. I will find places for you to stay where you will always be safe from harm. The people of

Sovorotskina are good and kind people who will open their hearts and homes to you. After all, we share a kinship that cannot be broken over time or place."

There was much rejoicing all around as the Ds danced around showing their approval of King Gateskin's suggestion. They all agreed to follow him and the group back to the Land of Goodness and Light.

Hearing this, Mitteran added, "I am blessed to have been freed too with my family. I promise you all that I will assist our new King Gateskin in getting you settled in our new home."

Mitteran was as happy as the Ds were to be going to a new peaceful place which they all could call home.

A CELEBRATION OF LIFE AND LOVE

CHAPTER 52

Queen Solinara was busy scurrying around preparing for the return of her family and the new visitors once she received word from King Gateskin that the group of Ds would be heading home soon along with their children and her brother and his wife. The Votovians were busy packing up their belongings and readying for their return to their homeland so they could make room for the Ds who would be staying in the extension until other arrangements could be made in the village.

The Votovian children were relieved to hear that Serena, Simon, Catalina and Spindle were all heroes and safely on their way home. There would be lots of adventurous stories to tell for many a day. Some of these stories would grow in exaggeration over the years but they would be enjoyed and believed by all. After all, the truth at times is truly unbelievable and cannot be exaggerated!

These children did not want to leave until they could see Serena, Simon, Catalina and Spindle for themselves. They wanted to hear about the boy, Arubane, and how he had come to be with the sheep. Serena had sent word that he was a very young but powerful wizard in his own right. They couldn't believe that he could perform the Transformation Spell all by himself. Most of them did not know how to do even the simple spells yet at ten years of age.

It was not long after Queen Solinara had gotten word the large group was heading their way through the forest that she opened the enchanted barrier in the trees. As Queen Solinara watched from the doorway of the cottage her heart beat furiously and she could not hold herself back any longer. She ran toward the trees as she spotted her husband and children passing through the barrier now glowing red.

King Gateskin and the children saw Queen Solinara running toward them and they met her in a group embrace. Queen Solinara kissed and hugged each of her family tightly before releasing them at the cottage door.

"Oh, thank the gods for bringing you all back safe and unharmed," Queen Solinara exclaimed with grateful tears in her eyes.

King Gateskin smiled and replied, "No worries, my love. We are all fine. I promised you I would be back, didn't I?"

Solinara smiled through her tears, "Yes, I guess you did say that. But I didn't expect to have to worry about both you and our children at the same time." She gave her husband another hug and she wiped her tears away.

Queen Solinara embraced each D as she welcomed them into her home. At the end of the group were her brother and sister-in-law walking side by side holding onto a little boy's hand. The little boy looked very much like Hotenfaran with his cloak and hat. As the three of them came closer, Queen Solinara noticed the boy's brilliant blue eyes were a duplicate of Procelina's eyes. Queen Solinara had never seen eyes like her sister-in-law's until now. It certainly was a surprise to her. It was almost as if this child was born from Hotenfaran and Procelina. This revelation shook Queen Solinara deeply and she felt tears in her eyes as she gazed upon the happy threesome. She hugged them in turn welcoming them home.

"Thank you for all that you did to bring my family home safely, Hotenfaran and Procelina! It is so good to see you. Is this your handsome son, Arubane?"

Arubane bowed to his aunt and spoke up, "Yes, it is I, Arubane, at your service, my aunt, Queen Solinara!"

He stepped forward and raised his arms to hug her. Solinara smiled at him and welcomed him into her arms for a huge hug. She looked over at her brother and sister-in-law and winked.

Hotenfaran and Procelina couldn't help but feel pride and love bursting out of them as they nodded back to Solinara.

***

Serena, Simon, Catalina and Spindle quickly shared the stories of their rescue adventures with the Votovian children as the Votovian men and women gathered their packs and headed out to the wagons to place all their belongings for the trip back home. Parting was hard for the children and adults who had been waiting for the return of the King and his children. They did not want to leave but knew that it was time to go. The Votovians would always be there to aid King Gateskin and his Village of Sovorotskina if he ever needed them again.

King Gateskin thanked King Cavelin and Queen Savina and all the people of Votovia for helping them out and watching over Queen Solinara and all the citizens of Sovorotskina and the other villages. King Gateskin said, "I could not have protected the villages without your help. I am eternally grateful to you and promise to be there for you if you ever need my assistance one day."

There was a chattering heard that was growing louder as the Votovians were gathering outside to head out on their journey home. The Sprites were all around standing high up on the branches of the trees sending up a cheer to the Votovians for their assistance in keeping everyone safe.

Abason and Anabal came rushing forward as the couple flew from the tallest tree and landed gracefully on the walk next to King Gateskin and his family. They both grasped the hands of King Gateskin in gratitude for the safe return of their son, Spindle. "We can't thank you enough, King Gateskin for bringing our son back safe and sound."

"I couldn't have done it if not for Spindle's and your help along the way."

Abason bowed to the King and said, "It was my pleasure to help. We are always here for you, my King, whenever you need us."

"Thank you, Abason. I may very well need you in the near future once again."

Spindle stepped forward and wrapped his arms around his parents. Anabal cried and sniffled as she hugged her son tightly, afraid to let him go. Abason shook his son's hand then also pulled him into a tight embrace. Abason was content to see his son's smiling face again. He had feared he would lose Spindle to the EOs as he had lost his brother so long ago.

"I am just fine, father. All is well. We had a great adventure. I will tell you all about it." Spindle couldn't help keep the excitement out of his voice over all that had transpired.

"I want to hear every word, my son. I am very proud of you. You showed great courage and fortitude," Abason said to his son in a voice that cracked with emotion.

King Gateskin announced, "Abason, I must tell you that Spindle was extremely brave and resourceful. I would not have been rescued without his assistance. Also, I must reiterate that I am extremely grateful to you and your fellow Sprites for all that you and they did to aid us in our adventure to the Land of Darkness and Evil. The Sprites were clever and organized and delightfully dexterous and glibly facile. We had a good laugh at some of their antics in scaring away the Parotovinan guards, eh, Spindle?"

King Gateskin laughed and winked at Spindle much to the delight of Abason and the other Sprites who gave a loud cheer in unison. Joy could be tangibly felt in the air all around them as the celebrating had just begun.

Spindle stepped closer to his father to share something. "Father, I wanted to find Uncle Micah but didn't know where to look. Things got so hectic that we had to leave as soon as we could. I'm sorry."

"Oh, Spindle. Don't worry about that. I guess it was not meant to be that Micah would return home. I have come to accept that, my son. You did more than enough for your King." Abason put his arm around Spindle's shoulder and hugged him as they walked away.

***

Queen Solinara, along with the other D women, conjured up a feast for all. They set up the tables in the extension and made room for everyone to eat, including the Votovians who were outside ready to travel home. Queen Solinara insisted that they stay long enough to partake of the feast and celebration before they begin their journey home. She set more long tables outside to accommodate them.

There was music and dancing and the children gathered together to talk about their adventures to the Land of Darkness much to the delight of the other children. Serena, Simon and Catalina even performed a few of the spells from Hotenfaran's Book of Spells and promised to teach some of the older children to do a spell or two.

Hotenfaran and Procelina had finally released Arubane's hands so he could join the other children. The children all wanted to hear about his performing the Transformation Spell from a sheep to a little boy. They all listened in awe of him and he was accepted quickly as a friend of the group.

Hotenfaran and Procelina stood away from the group but could hear everything that was spoken and smiled happily as they watched their newfound son tell his tales of spells and wizardry. The emptiness they once had felt was now completely filled by the joy of having Arubane as their son. They both looked forward to teaching Arubane everything they knew and giving him, the abundance of love they had kept inside for so long.

There was a little Sprite man who was outside the group of Ds who was observing, and seemed a little reticent to join in the celebrating. He was a very small Sprite with green hair and a tanned face with brown pants, shirt and cloak.

He was quite serious as he walked over to Abason, Anabal and Spindle who were talking together excitedly. As he waited for a break in their conversation, he cleared his throat, readying himself to speak.

Abason turned when he heard someone come up behind him. As he turned to look at the man who was standing there, Abason let out a cry of surprise. He grabbed the man in a hug saying over and over again, "Oh you are here, you are here; you finally came back!"

Anabal and Spindle looked at the two Sprite men hugging and crying. They suddenly realized that this man was Abason's long lost brother, Micah. They waited until the men stopped crying and talking as one before they too stepped forward to greet Micah.

"Ah, Anabal, you are as lovely as I remember you when I was just a little boy. You were a lovely little girl back then. If I had not left, I may have married you myself."

Anabal laughed at her brother-in-law's words. She remembered Micah well but did not want to tell him that she only had eyes for Abason even as a child. She had always loved Abason as Abason had always loved Anabal. Abason smiled at his wife as he still held tightly to his brother. He felt so much love for his family and now it was complete to have his brother back in the fold. They had a lot to talk about and needed to make up for all the lost time apart.

Spindle waited for his turn to greet his uncle and shook Micah's hand in greeting. Micah laughed at his nephew's formal greeting but shook Spindle's hand tightly and then hugged and patted Spindle on the back saying, "I am deeply grateful to you, Spindle, for helping to rescue me from the Land of Darkness and Evil. I never thought I would leave that dreadful place. I am so happy to be back here in my homeland. We have a lot to talk about, my nephew. I need to get to know you and my brother and sister-in-law. I have been away too long. But I must first introduce you to my family too. Micah extended his hand out to a diminutive lovely Sprite woman and alongside her walked two children, a boy of five and a girl of eight. They were enveloped by their newfound family and welcomed to go back to the tree homes to get settled.

Abason exchanged smiles with his son and said, "I guess it was meant to be after all that Micah would come home. You did your part to make this possible, my son. Thank you."

Spindle shrugged his shoulders and was speechless. All he could do was nod to his father as tears threatened to appear.

Abason patted Spindle on the back and went to his brother who was waiting for him with his family.

The Sprites, all but Spindle, excused themselves from the King and the group and went back to their homes to make a place for Micah and his family in their own new tree home next to Abason's. Abason had readied this tree home many years ago hoping and anticipating his brother, Micah's, return one day.

They had much to discuss about all the years that Micah had been gone. They looked forward to hearing about his adventures and how he survived all those year in the Land of Darkness.

CHAPTER 53

After the Sprites moved away, a man stepped forward and waited to speak to the King. He had stayed at the back of the group as they passed through the trees after the spell was broken. He was hesitant about disturbing King Gateskin but he knew he must talk to him.

"Excuse me, King Gateskin. May I speak with you?"

"Oh Botular. I forgot all about you. Did you hear anything in the woods?"

"No, good King, all was quiet. But I wanted to tell you that I noticed how happy everyone is here in Sovorotskina. Have you given any thought to my becoming a citizen of your beautiful village?" Botular pleaded with the King as he bowed once again.

"Ah yes, Botular. I have given it much thought. I see that you followed us through the boundary safely. Do you really want to become a citizen? Are you sure you don't want to return to your homeland of Parotovina?"

"Oh yes, I want to become a citizen more than anything in this world. Please accept me, a humble servant of yours."

Gateskin placed his hand on Botular's head and patted it. "Please stand up, Botular. I need to look into your eyes when you say this. Please say it again."

Botular stood up shakily and looked King Gateskin in the eye and announced strongly and firmly, "Yes, I want to become a citizen of your beautiful land of Sovorotskina. Please! I will do whatever you need me to do, my King. I am your servant."

Gateskin snickered and shook Botular's hand. "So, it shall be declared tomorrow with all the others who want this too. We will have a ceremony and pronounce you, along with many others, new citizens of Sorovotskina."

Botular bowed and kissed the King's shoe and thanked him again and again for his kindness. "I don't know what I can do to repay you for this honor, King Gateskin, but I will do whatever it takes to earn your trust and become a true and good citizen of this land."

The guard neglected to tell King Gateskin that he had tried to reach his own King to report he had stumbled upon King Gateskin's three children. At the time he did this he had not received a message back from the Parotovinan King. But now he could feel some words coming into his head from his King and he was not happy.

"I'm sure you will, Botular. I can see in your eyes that you are a good and decent man." King Gateskin stopped in mid-thought when he noticed Botular's face had gone white.

"What is wrong, Botular? Is there something you need to tell me?"

"I…um…I forgot to mention that I sent a message to King Parotovina back at the cave. But I didn't think it went through. Now he just contacted me and wants me to return to the village right away with…"

"With what, Botular?" King Gateskin asked in a strong voice that made Botular jump back in alarm.

"I…I'm sorry, Your Highness. I didn't know I would meet you and…"

"Get to the point, Botular! What did he want you to return with?" Gateskin's face was scarlet with anger which would only increase until the guard answered his question.

"Please forgive me, King Gateskin. I would never have caused them harm. I was only trying to save my own skin. I know the King would want to kill me if I didn't have something to offer him."

"What are you trying to tell me, Botular? Spit it out now before I banish you back to your King."

"Yes, yes, of course. I promised him I would bring your children to him. He asked me to turn them to his ways by using a special incantation created by his wizards. They were to instruct me how to do this. But I didn't do that."

"What? What did you say? You can't be serious! Now you want to be a citizen of my village after this! You threaten my children with harm and try to turn them to your evil ways!"

"Yes, but I wouldn't have done that. I only had to give the King something to get him off my back. The other guards would have told him I was a deserter if I hadn't done that. I will do whatever I can to earn your trust, my king. Please tell me what I can do to make amends."

"There will be much you will need to do to show that you are sincere before you will be considered for citizenship."

"I understand, King Gateskin. Please forgive me. I would never have done that terrible thing." Botular hung his head and cried. His shoulders shook so violently that he collapsed in a heap.

When the King saw the state Botular was in, he picked up the guard and led him to his home.

"Thank you, King Gateskin. I am truly sorry. I will not answer King Kaposkaran. He will never know if I received his message or not. I will do all I can to make up for this awful thing that I should not have done." Botular continued to sniffle as he walked along with the King.

"I want to believe you, Botular. You will work hard to earn my trust I will make sure and at that time it will be my honor to call you a fellow citizen of our Land of Goodness and Light. Now, come into my home and get comfortable. I want to introduce you to my wife, Queen Solinara. She will be happy to meet you finally, if I am correct."

Botular looked up at the King and said, "Finally?"

Solinara was in the kitchen doing her magic to help things along. There were so many new people in her home to feed and offer a place to stay until all was settled in the morning. She looked up when she saw Gateskin standing there with his hand on the shoulder of a tall man, almost her husband's height of well over six and a half feet, who was avoiding looking into her eyes. She gasped when he looked up at her.

"Botular? Is that really you?"

The man smiled and went to meet his new Queen who took him into her arms unexpectedly and held him tightly.

Gateskin stood aside and looked puzzled. Who was this man? How did his wife know him? He thought back to her cryptic message.

Botular was puzzled too. He didn't know why the Queen had hugged him and acted as if she knew him.

Solarina smiled and began to explain, "I'm sorry Botular. I couldn't help being excited to see you. I realize that you wouldn't know me. I saw your parents in a dream. They told me about you and asked that I try to find you and bring you home to Sovorotskina."

Gateskin smiled and said, "Ah yes. Now I understand what you meant in the letter you told the children to give me. It said, 'Find him and bring him back here. You will find him in the cave. That did cross my mind at the time I met Botular."

Botular looked confused and asked, "How did you know my parents, my Queen?"

"I didn't really know them. They somehow came to me in my dreams. I don't know how they did that. They must have been extremely powerful to do that. I saw them many years ago in a dream and then forgot about them until they came to me again recently in a daydream. They were more urgent this time that I must find you and bring you back to their homeland of Sovorotskina. They were TOs. They even showed me a photo of you and told me your name. I didn't know how to find you until they told me where. That is why I told Gateskin to find you in the cave and bring you back home."

Gateskin sniggered, "You expected me to figure out what you meant by that cryptic message, my love? I didn't know what you meant. At first, I thought you meant our children who were in the cave. But you did say, *him*. I did finally figure that this man could be to whom you were referring."

"Well, it did all work out, didn't it? Now Botular is safe here in the homeland of his parents. It is wonderful to meet you, Botular. Welcome to Sovorotskina," Queen Solinara said with a warm smile and a sparkle to her eyes.

Botular bowed to his Queen and King. They pointed the way so he could join the others at the table. After seeing the wonderful spread, he realized, he was starving.

Queen Solinara watched her husband's expression as he observed Botular making himself comfortable at the table with the others.

"What's wrong, Gateskin?"

"Nothing, my love. Everything is okay now. I was concerned about something but nothing for you to worry about."

Solinara arched her brow at her husband and said, "Really?" She shook her head and went to the table to assist her guests but not before giving her husband a steely look.

Gateskin met her gaze with a smile and a wink to ease her concern. He hoped that would work for now. She would eventually keep asking him the same question until he told her. This, he could not do. He could not share what Botular had confessed to him.

CHAPTER 54

The celebration went on into the early morning hours before it finally quieted down as each family retired to their beds and the Votovians finally headed out on their journey home. King Cavelan and Queen Savina planned to fly the whole group home under cover of the Invisible Curtain Spell since everyone was very tired from being up all night. The youngest children were safely tucked into the wagons sound asleep as were the older Votovians. The young adult Votovians were in charge of keeping watch over the rest as they flew home, which gave a much-appreciated boost to the young adults' egos.

King Cavelan and Queen Savina bade goodbye to King Gateskin and Queen Solinara. King Cavelan said, "Thank you so much for being so warm and inviting to us in your home. We will keep in touch and, if needed, we will be here for you always."

Gateskin nodded and shared hugs with them both. Queen Savina hugged Queen Solinara tightly and said her own thanks, "It has been a pleasure to spend time with you, Solinara. You were the perfect hostess. As for your question, yes, we are descendants of Noella I."

Queen Solinara smiled and hugged Queen Savina back and chuckled, "I didn't realize you could read my thoughts."

"You'd be surprised what we women can do, dear Solinara. We even sent vibes to you to help calm you down. I think it worked somewhat, don't you?"

"Yes, my friend. I think it did. Thank you. I look forward to seeing you again in better circumstances."

"Yes, that I would like too, Solinara."

The Votovians waved goodbye one last time to King Gateskin and Queen Solinara who watched them as they flew over Sovorotskina.

***

Suddenly a multitude of oinks were heard as everyone who had settled down to sleep jumped out of their beds, still groggy, and looked out the windows of the house at a numerous number of pigs sitting in the yard looking back at them. These pigs had evidently wandered off after coming through the barrier of the trees when it was opened along with the others. The pigs had managed to move around without anyone seeing them to forage for something to eat. They had thereafter ended up in the area of the cottage and extension.

Serena, Simon and Catalina, too excited to sleep, heard the ruckus and rushed forward to explain to their parents and everyone else what had happened. Procelina and Hotenfaran, also now awake, stepped outside and raised their hands over the pigs and the Parotovinan scouting party appeared.

Shocked expressions were on everyone's faces and also on the faces of the Parotovinans. King Gateskin stepped forward to talk to the men.

"I'm sorry this was done to you but it was necessary to save the lives of many. I think it would be best if you return to your homes and leave us. But first, you must not share any of this with King Kaposkaran. Can you promise to do this?" King Gateskin knew, though, that they could not be trusted.

The men exchanged looks and nodded. One man stepped forward to speak. He bowed to King Gateskin and said, "It is an honor to meet you, King Gateskin. I am a descendant of the TOs. I would prefer to stay here in your land. I do not have any family back in Parotovina."

Some of the other men stepped forward too and explained they wanted to stay also. There were several more that did not express this sentiment since they had families left behind.

"I see. You are all welcome to stay but you must take an oath of honor and become Sovorotskinans. The rest of you can leave. I will not harm you. I will erase your memories so you won't be able to tell your king about this meeting."

The men nodded, turned and walked away through the opening of the Tree Enchantment Spell after King Gateskin wiped their memories for safekeeping. He gathered the others who wanted to stay and welcomed them. "I will have a ceremony tomorrow, well really today, but after we have all had some sleep, for you to become citizens of this land. In the meantime, I will provide shelter and food for you in my home."

The men cried and thanked King Gateskin over and over by shaking his hand and bowing down before him. They said, "We can't thank you enough, King Gateskin. We are finally free. We are truly grateful to you for your kindness. Such kindness we have never known."

Gateskin shook each man's hand and welcomed them into his home to introduce them to his family and provide food after their long journey.

Soon everyone was settled once again for the night for some much-needed rest.

All was safe in the Land of Goodness and Light…but not for long…

***

Gateskin couldn't sleep until after he had checked on his children again. He couldn't get out of his mind what Botular had said. He tiptoed into Simon's room first and saw his face serene in sleep. Next, he opened his girls' door and crept closer to look down on Catalina. She was such a sweet little girl. He kept calling her little but she was blossoming and would soon be too grown up to be called a little girl anymore.

He leaned over Serena's twin bed against the opposite wall and jumped back when she opened her eyes to him.

"Father, what's wrong? Why are you in here? Has something happened?"

"No, no, everything is okay, sweetheart. I just wanted to make sure you are all safe. It was a harrowing adventure and I felt fortunate we all returned unharmed."

"I know that is not all, Father. I can read your mind, you know. There is something else in there that is bothering you. It has to do with the man who you were talking to earlier. He was the guard we found at the cave. What did he say to upset you?"

Gateskin looked at his daughter in amazement. She was getting more powerful with each day to be able to see inside the deepest recesses of his mind. He thought he had safely tucked his concerns there so Solinara would not see them. He had forgotten Serena was able to see further than even her mother at this stage of her developing powers.

He sighed and responded, "I'm sorry, Serena. I did not want to tell your mother and certainly not you any of this. It was quite upsetting."

Serena sat up and waited. "Please, father, continue. I assure you I can handle whatever it is."

Gateskin looked with love at his eldest child. "I think you are the strongest of my children, Serena, and can handle anything that is thrown at you including this."

Serena smiled and patted her father's hand encouraging him to continue.

"Botular told me he had contacted King Kaposkaran about bringing you and your siblings back to the Land of Darkness. He was supposed to put a spell over you three to turn you to the evil ways of the King."

Serena didn't say anything for a few minutes. She looked up at her father. "Botular did try to do that spell but I stopped him from continuing. He is not to be trusted. I think he is a spy, Father, for his king. I will keep a close eye on him. I have not told Simon or Catalina about this though. I don't want them to be anxious around Botular."

"Good idea not to tell them. I will keep a close watch on him too, Serena." Gateskin shook his head in disbelief that Botular had lied to him. He had to ask his daughter, "How did you stop his spell?"

"I have been studying Mom's and Uncle Hotenfaran's Book of Spells daily. There is a spell in there that can stop another spell. It's called Disconnectus. It is supposed to interfere with a spell and make it ineffective or interrupt its function before it comes to fruition."

"Hmm, I see. I should read this book myself. I could learn a few things that could be helpful to me. What do you think?"

"Oh, you are so funny, Father. You don't need to learn anything. You know everything that is important. I think what happened was you wanted to believe in Botular because of the message Mother gave you."

"How did you know about the message? You couldn't read it." Gateskin was puzzled and more in awe of his powerful daughter.

"Not too hard to do, Father. I listened into your mind and read the message later on. You kept running it around in your head because you were confused about its meaning. I figured it out after you met Botular. He was the only one, other than us, in the cave at that time."

Gateskin chuckled softly so as not to wake Catalina. "Yes, I see, my lovely and brilliant daughter. Yes, I see! Well, you better get some sleep. Now I feel as if I will too. Thank you, Serena. Good night."

He leaned over and kissed her cheek and patted her covers around her like he used to do when she was just a child.

"Thanks, Father. Good night. I love you." Serena snuggled into her bed and smiled in contentment.

"I love you too, Serena." Gateskin tiptoed out of the room and headed back to his room where his wife was sitting up waiting for him.

"What's going on, Gateskin?"

The King groaned and sighed heavily.

A DANGEROUS ADVENTURE BEGINS

CHAPTER 55

Back in the Land of Evil and Darkness the guards had finally reached the gate of the Village of Parotovina the following afternoon. The Gatekeeper awoke to hear the three guards knocking on his shed to gain entrance to the village.

The guards were agitated and tired from their long trip back and very apprehensive about what the King would say to them. They asked the Gatekeeper, "Did Mitteran arrive yet?"

"No, I have not seen him. The only ones I saw were the two shepherds and their flock of many sheep leaving the village and heading north."

The guards exchanged surprised looks back and forth without saying anything to the Gatekeeper about that.

Instead, they requested, "Let us in. We have news for the King that we are sure he would want to hear."

The gate was opened. As the guards walked into the Village of Evil and Darkness, they noticed it was very quiet and no one was out and about. They quickly went to the castle to gain entrance to request an audience with King Kaposkaran.

The guards who were in charge of guarding the King and his castle stood to attention as they cautiously watched the four wandering, bedraggled guards heading toward them. The castle guards did not know what to make of these men, ill kempt and dirty, dressed in the uniforms of Parotovinan guards. The castle guards were prepared for the worst and would defend their King and his castle to the death.

The four tired guards gingerly approached the castle guards and explained, "We are under the command of Mitteran and are here to speak to the King. We have news of utmost importance for King Kaposkaran."

The castle guards shook their heads at the four misfit guards. "We can not let you in. You do not have an appointment to meet with the King."

This refusal caused Mitteran's four guards' tempers to flare and they began to argue with the castle guards loud enough for the King himself to hear in his dining room.

The King called out to the castle guards. "What is all that noise about? Who is disturbing my meal?"

One of the castle guards went to speak with the King to explain the disruption and to calm the

King down while the other guard kept the misfits at bay. The castle guards were very fearful of the King when he was angered, for he was known to kill anyone who caused him any grief even if it was a minor infraction.

"What is the meaning of this interruption? Don't you see that I am trying to enjoy my early morning meal? What is going on out there? Can't you two handle anything without constant supervision by me?" King Kaposkaran's eyes looked like steel globes of anger at the castle guard standing in front of him. The King noticed the fear in his guard's eyes and smiled to himself for this discomfort brought the King a measure of pleasure to see the guard so fearful.

"I…I… I'm so sorry, Your Highness. It seems that there are four of Mitteran's guards who just arrived. They insist on meeting with you. They say they have some news of utmost importance to you. I will send them away, I promise you, King Kaposkaran." The castle guard shook from fear as he backed his way quickly out of the King's dining room before he could be struck down by the King's anger.

"Stop right where you are, you imbecile! What do you mean these guards have news for me? Where is Mitteran? He has not returned. Where are the TOs that he promised me? Where is King Gateskin? Mitteran promised he had King Gateskin in his hands and was bringing him to me."

The King did not wait for his castle guard to reply but instead the King marched out of his dining room roughly pushing his guard aside to find out what news Mitteran's guards had for him. The King stood in the foyer of his castle eyeing the four grungy-looking guards standing in front of the castle guard who was holding them at arms' length with his sword.

King Kaposkaran called out to the second castle guard. "Send these men into my meeting room now."

The second castle guard jumped to attention and escorted the four misfit guards to the King's meeting room and then went back to his station at the front of the castle door. When he got back to his station, he almost ran into the first castle guard who had been dismissed by the King. The guard's face was deathly pale and he looked as if he was going to faint, be sick or both. The second guard tried to ask the first guard what had happened to frighten him so but the man could not talk and just shook all over.

The four dirty and exhausted guards stood at attention in the King's meeting room as King Kaposkaran paced back and forth in front of them. The guards first explained, "Mitteran took King Gateskin out to the forest and then all chaos had broken out from the loud booming noise as we ran around trying to figure out if we were being attacked."

The guards then told the King, "On our way back to find Mitteran we saw two shepherds and many sheep traveling to the cave of Crotesia Mountain. There were loud sounds that we had heard before and felt that kept us from reaching the cave as we tried to follow the shepherds and the flock of sheep."

The King became deathly quiet. His face took on a serious demeanor as he thought this news over carefully. The King turned to face the bedraggled guards to give them a new order. "I want you four to lead ten of my top guards back to the cave and surprise the shepherds and their flock and bring them all back to me. You are to find Mitteran and King Gateskin and bring them back here too. Do you understand? If you do not come back with them, you will be killed along with your families? Do I make myself clear?"

The four guards just nodded and were told, "Now get out of my sight, get cleaned up and ready to travel. Come back to the castle within half an hour to meet the ten other guards who will be waiting for you."

The guardsmen quickly left the castle to return to their homes to get cleaned up and refreshed. They feared for their lives and the lives of their families but knew they had to succeed in completing King Kaposkaran's orders. The guards tried to assure their families that they would return with the shepherds and their flock, Mitteran and King Gateskin as the King had commanded them. But if by some chance they did not succeed, the guards told their wives to take themselves and the children and hide away until they could find a way to get out of the Land of Evil and Darkness on their own away from the King's wrath.

The King, in the meantime, called some of his most powerful wizards and sorcerers together in his meeting room to discuss the news he had just received.

The wizards had noted, "The village is strangely empty of people. There are no children's voices heard playing around the yards and no animal sounds."

The wizards and sorcerers shared their thoughts with their King. "We think that magic must have been performed changing some of the Parotovinan citizens into sheep."

The King mused, "This explained the shepherds leading out such a multitude of sheep from the village that the three guards relayed to me."

The King gave his wizards the order. "You will bring the Head Guard to the square and kill him. He was responsible for letting the shepherds into the village and then allowing them to leave with all the sheep. Someone will have to pay for this!" the King exclaimed loudly to this powerful group of wizards and sorcerers.

He knew these wizards and sorcerers were powerful enough to kill him too. But the King kept these powerful men at bay by treating them almost as equals and allowing them to live in his castle. The King also kept a careful watch over these magical people by threatening to put their families in the castle dungeon if any of them ever turned on him.

Soon after the King's decree, a high-pitched scream was heard all over the kingdom as the Gatekeeper was first tortured then put to death in the square by the power of the wizards. What few citizens were left, kept their families locked behind their cottage doors to try to keep out the Gatekeeper's screams.

Sprites all around the forest bordering the village whispered amongst themselves over what was happening to the Gatekeeper. They knew what they must do.

***

Back in Sovorotskina the next morning…

Spindle knocked on the King's door. Once he answered, Spindle stepped closer to King

411

Gateskin and cleared his throat to get his attention.

King Gateskin looked down on Spindle and asked, "What is it, my good little man? You look upset."

"I must speak to Hotenfaran right away. I have some bad news to share."

Gateskin called Hotenfaran, who was sitting having breakfast with his family, over, "Please come here for a moment. Spindle has something important to share with you."

"What is it, Spindle?" Hotenfaran bent down to Spindle's level to hear what he had to say. He could tell by the Sprite's disturbed look that it was not going to be good news.

"I received an urgent message from the Sprites surrounding the land of Parotovina. They asked me to share this with you right away." Spindle shuffled his feet and looked at the ground before continuing.

"Oh, my little man. What's wrong? What could possibly be the matter? We are all safe, well and celebrating."

"I know. I'm sorry to have to tell you this but the man you helped in the road on our travels, Kelleran, the Gatekeeper, was taken away and punished for letting you pass with the sheep. They tortured him and then hung him in the square as a warning to the rest of the citizens."

Hotenfaran held his breath and bowed his head. "Oh no, poor Kelleran! I'm sorry for his family. We must get them out of there. They will be next. Kelleran was a kind man. I never even thought that would happen. Their king is truly evil. He rules his kingdom with fear. I feel somewhat responsible for his demise. I wish I could have done something to prevent this. Maybe we should have taken him with us along with the sheep." Hotenfaran hung his head and sighed deeply rubbing his brow.

"I will help you, great wizard! I will go with you and have my fellow Sprites help us get the Gatekeeper's family out safely."

"Thank you, Spindle, you are a brave young man. I would appreciate your help and that of your fellow Sprites. I must inform King Gateskin of our plans and of course, my wife." Hotenfaran rolled his eyes at Spindle which made the Sprite smile and hold back a snicker.

King Gateskin listened to Hotenfaran's plan and agreed. He would go with them and take several of his guards along. He asked Spindle not to share this trip with his children. He knew they would be compelled to go with them. He didn't feel like arguing with his daughter Serena again.

Mitteran was standing nearby and heard the exchange. He joined in and said, "I'm sorry but I overheard what you said, Hotenfaran. I want to help too. I knew Kelleran well. He was an exemplary guard and caring man. He didn't deserve what happened to him."

"Thank you, Mitteran. But you don't need to do this. You have your family to care for," Gateskin exclaimed.

"No, I must come with you. I know the layout of the village and where Kelleran's family lives.

You need me. Don't worry about my family. They are safely here now. My wife would expect nothing less of me. She will understand."

"All right, Mitteran. Thank you for offering to come. I think you are correct. We do need you. We have no idea where Kelleran's family lives. We would have wasted a lot of time trying to find them."

Mitteran nodded and ran off to tell his wife what he was about to do. He only hoped she would be as understanding as he said she would be.

The King did the same. After explaining to Queen Solinara about his plans, she promised, "Don't worry, Gateskin. I will keep the children busy under a spell to keep your thoughts from escaping and being heard by them."

But the children up and about were already listening in the other room and were making plans of their own unbeknownst to their parents.

King Gateskin and the rescue party would leave as soon as possible to find Kelleran's family and bring them to safety. They were sure that this time the EOs would be ready for them. The rescue party would need all the help they could get and more magic than they ever had to use before.

CHAPTER 56

Serena instructed her siblings to gather some supplies and meet her in the woods in the back of their house before their mother came back.

"How are we going to get out through Mother's spell at the border of the woods?" Simon asked with a puzzled look on his face.

"Don't worry, I have an idea. We will follow closely behind Father, his guardsmen, Uncle Hotenfaran, Mitteran and Spindle. I will whisper into Spindle's ear that we are coming along and request he doesn't tell Father. I know he will not betray me. He will make sure that we are safely out before the border closes with Mother's spell."

"I hope you are right, Serena," Simon mused as he shook his head at his sister's crazy idea.

"Don't worry, Simon. I will help you," Catalina exclaimed in a strong voice belying her anxiety.

Simon smiled at his younger sister and patted her on the head. "Thank you, Catalina. But I think I can take care of myself just fine." When he saw the disappointment registered on her little face he explained, "Of course, Catalina. I think I may need your expert help with spells and stuff. Stay close to me, little sister."

Catalina smiled, happily grabbed her brother's hand and gave it a grateful squeeze. She adjusted her backpack and walked alongside her brother with pride.

As the border closed in the trees, Solinara gasped when she spotted her three children once again escaping to join the rescue party. She could see them even through the spell Serena had put over them to make them invisible. This spell became clear to her as the children passed through the border and came into contact with her spell as the trees opened up.

She sent word to her husband that he must keep them safe as before. He promised nothing less. He turned to look behind him but the children were still invisible from a spell most certainly conjured by Serena, he surmised. He smiled to himself feeling proud of his children and picked up the pace.

Spindle looked back to see if Serena and her siblings were close behind but he couldn't see them. He whispered, "Serena, are you there?"

"Shh, we are here, Spindle. I don't want my father to see us just yet. Of course, unless my mother somehow saw us already. She would have warned Father. I don't want to take off the spell just yet. Give us a little time to get farther ahead on the path before he tries to send us back. If we get out of Sovorotskina then he will not feel safe sending us back alone."

"Oh yes, I see. Good idea, Serena. You are quite clever. I wish I had thought of that. Don't worry

I will protect you all along with my fellow Sprites. We will come up with something tricky to scare any EOs away."

There was a chattering heard in the trees as the Sprites agreed with Spindle.

"See, I told you. They have something in the wind to try," Spindle chortled.

Gateskin was listening in on their whisperings and snickered to himself. There would be time to discuss this with his children once again. He couldn't help feeling proud of them for their bravery, persistence and insistence on helping with another rescue attempt. He would make sure they were kept safe as before, even if he had to hogtie them down to do it.

The King looked over his shoulder once again to see if his children were now visible since they were crossing over the river named after him and then into the border of Merona. He wanted to take a different route to Parotovina by way of Merona, then Merlina and over the border of Parotovina. He planned to enter the woods behind the village and use some of his magic to fool the guards so that they could enter safely.

He knew his daughter, Serena, had many powers and knew some spells that would help him do this.

Unbeknownst to Gateskin, Serena was reading his thoughts and chuckling too. She sent a message to her father – *I will be more than happy to assist you, Father!*

Gateskin responded, *Thank you, my daughter. We will discuss this later in more detail about your coming along and also about the spells.*

Yes, Father. Serena smiled in contentment that now she knew her father wasn't angry with her. Well, not completely anyway. She breathed a sigh of relief.

What Serena wasn't telling her father was that she kept getting strange messages in her head that were evil in nature. She didn't like the feelings they were emitting inside her. She did all she could to turn them away. She was beginning to think that the Disconnectus Spell really didn't work after all. This spell interrupted messages and then blocked them from coming through her mind. The messages kept coming more furiously the further away she was from her home of

Sovorotskina. She felt fear for once in her life. What was she to do?

Gateskin didn't let on but he could feel his daughter's anxiety level rising. He was concerned and would have to contact her and find out what was bothering her. She never lost her composure in the toughest situations. He was deeply concerned something was terribly wrong. Could it have something to do with what Botular told him about his King?

After their talk that night in Serena's bedroom she had promised to keep a close eye on Botular for any signs that he was keeping in touch with King Kaposkaran. If he was, she was to contact Gateskin immediately so he could put a stop to it. He now carried a supply of Staglemite that Hotenfaran had treated to make it work one way only for curtailing messages.

He would have to share this fact with Serena soon for she was getting more upset, the further away they got from Sovorotskina. What would happen when they arrived at the Land of Evil and Darkness? He didn't want to see his daughter go to the dark ways of the King.

Serena was struggling to keep her mind clear of these evil messages but they were becoming stronger by the minute. She dropped the Invisible Curtain Spell over her siblings and herself to see if she could concentrate better on the messages to dispel them from her mind.

Gateskin stopped the party from moving forward by raising his fist. They looked at one another in bewilderment as they waited to hear why the King had put a halt to their march.

The guardsmen stood to attention waiting for further instructions from their King.

King Gateskin whispered, "It's okay. Just sit tight. I need to speak with my daughter."

The guardsmen nodded and stood close by in case they were needed.

The others in the rescue party were unaware that the King's children were accompanying them on this trip. They turned to observe the King as he went to the end of the troop to speak with Serena who had suddenly appeared with her siblings.

"Serena, are you all right?" Gateskin whispered in concern with furrowed brows.

"Yes, Father. I think so. But…"

"What? What is the matter, Serena? Please tell me." Serena shook her head at first but then she suddenly collapsed at her father's feet.

Spindle rushed to Serena's side next to King Gateskin. He sat beside her with deep anxiety on his little brown face which had now turned nearly white in fright.

"Serena!" Gateskin bent down and picked up his daughter. Her face was pale, her body stiff and she was unconscious. He was shocked but tried to stay calm as he worked to bring his daughter back. He waved his hand over her forehead and tuned into her thoughts. What he saw there was disturbing. No wonder she had passed out.

He had carried some Pepper Salts in his pocket that when crushed in his hands and waved under one's nose, would awaken anyone from a coma. He took a small portion and did just that to Serena. She jumped out of her comatose state with a shocked expression on her face.

"What happened, Father? Did I pass out?"

"Yes, you did, Serena. I awakened you with Pepper Salts that your Uncle Hotenfaran gave me. I didn't think we would need them but I guess I was wrong. Are you all right now? What's going on, Serena. Please tell me."

"I...I thought the spell was broken. I didn't think they would be able to get through. But they are sending me disturbing messages and pictures now which is why I passed out. These pictures are quite terrible to explain. Please don't make me share what I saw. It was too horrible! It makes me sick to my stomach."

"It's okay, Serena. Take your time and get settled. But you must share what the messages are with me and me alone. No one else has to know."

"Yes, I think I better tell you, Father. It's important. The evil King Kaposkaran is trying to turn me to his evil ways by sending me these terrible messages of death and revenge. He says he is going to kill us all. We must not go any further. I fear for the lives of everyone here." Serena opened her mind to her father so he could see all the messages of evil.

Serena leaned closer to her father and whispered, "The photos he is showing me are of the Gatekeeper's dead body swinging from rafters in the square there. It is so awful to see. It must have caused me to faint. That was the only way I guess I could stop his messages and photos from coming into my mind. They have stopped for the time being. But I don't think King Kaposkaran will stop until he drives me crazy."

Gateskin had to make a decision right away to keep his daughter and the rest of the party safe. He turned to the front of the group and raised his hand to get their attention.

"Listen, I have received messages that put our lives in danger if we travel any further. We must return home right away. We can decide later when it would be safe to come back."

Mitteran stepped forward and asked, "But, King Gateskin, what about the Gatekeeper's family? We can't leave them there. King Kaposkaran will have them murdered because of Kelleran's betrayal to him."

"Yes, I understand. I want to take Kelleran's family safely out of Parotovina but not at the expense of the health of my daughter, Serena."

Hotenfaran asked with concern, "Is there something you need to tell us, King Gateskin? I can be of help if you need anything at all."

Gateskin looked at Hotenfaran and sent his concerns to his brother-in-law's mind, protected by the Staglemite, so that no one else could read them.

Hotenfaran nodded in agreement. "I agree, Your Highness. We must return home immediately and gather together for further consultations about this trip. I can see we may be in danger if we do not heed your request right away."

Mitteran looked puzzled but nodded and walked over to King Gateskin and patted him on the arm and said, "We will do whatever you wish of us, good King. We are at your disposal."

The guardsmen were instructed to lead the way home by their King. They never questioned their King but did his bidding. Their job was to protect the King and his family at all costs. That's what they did. They were always prepared to die for King Gateskin if necessary.

Gateskin shook Mitteran's outstretched hand in solidarity and began leading the group behind the guardsmen back to the safety of Sovorotskina.

***

Back in Parotovina King Kaposkaran smiled. He had succeeded in reaching the mind of Serena, the eldest daughter of King Gateskin, with the help of his powerful wizards. Serena was known to be gifted with great powers and could be most valuable to him if he could turn her to his ways. He would not give up until he had her in his village. She would be used to capture the control of the village of Sovorotskina and all its citizens including the King and Queen. Once the village of Sovorotskina fell, so would the other villages in succession. King Gateskin was the strongest and most powerful wizard of all of Noella Province.

Once King Kaposkaran had Serena in his power, he would rename the whole Province – Kaposkaran Province, once and for all. Then all the villages would be under his rule. He would be the richest and most powerful King. No one would be able to stop him.

The King cackled as he sat down to enjoy his meal and partake of his special wine to celebrate.

CHAPTER 57

Spindle followed the group back to Sovorotskina relieved now that Serena appeared to be feeling better. He was concerned about her welfare but could see King Gateskin didn't want to share whatever it was that was bothering his daughter.

He skipped his way over to the King and asked, "King Gateskin, can I be of service to you? What can I do to help Serena?"

"Thank you, Spindle. But Serena has recovered. She had a slight fainting spell. It could be from the heat or she is just hungry or tired. She has taken a drink and had some refreshments to help her gain her strength. But I still think it's best we return home for the time being."

"Yes, I understand, my King. Serena's health is much more important than anything else right now. But I can assist you in sending a message to Kelleran's family through my fellow Sprites who live outside the border of Parotovina."

"Ah, yes, Spindle. That would be most helpful. I'm glad you thought of this. You are quite an industrious young man. When we return to our village, I want to make you one of my guards officially, if that is okay with your parents. We will have a ceremony for the TOs too to make them citizens of Sovorotskina," King Gateskin announced as he shook Spindle's little hand gently and patted him lightly on the back in thanks.

"Thank you, my King. Now do you want me to speak with my fellow Sprites? What do you want me to tell them to do?"

"Well, let's see," King Gateskin smiled after contemplating for a minute or two and responded, "Why don't you tell them to go to Kelleran's home, get that location from Mitteran, and then instruct the family to run out into the woods and hide out with the Sprites until we can rescue them."

"Right away, my King." After Spindle got the location of Kelleran's home he raced over to the nearest trees and whispered to his fellow Sprites. They responded in a flurry and scurried off to pass the word throughout the trees until the message was delivered to the Sprites who lived the closest to Kelleran's cottage.

After Spindle did what King Gateskin asked, he walked next to Serena and took her hand. "Are you all right now, Serena? You really frightened me."

"Oh, Spindle, I'm fine. Just a fainting spell. Nothing to worry about."

Spindle looked at her with an arched brow. "What are you hiding, Serena? You know we are friends. You can share anything with me."

"I'm sorry, Spindle. But maybe later we can talk about this. Please understand. I can't share anything with you just yet. Okay? Thank you, though, for being such a good friend."

"Okay, Serena. But you know I am here for you whenever you need me." Spindle felt Serena squeeze his hand in thanks.

***

Safely back in Sovorotskina, King Gateskin gathered all the Ds of the TOs to the field in back of his house. Solinara had set up a stage with a podium, a high raised platform and seating areas for all once she received a message from Gateskin what his plans were to perform the Citizenship Ceremony upon his return. At the end of the ceremony, he would implement the adoption of Arubane.

"Please take a seat everyone so we can begin shortly. There will be refreshments afterwards."

Gateskin stepped aside to speak with Solinara to inform her of what had transpired, the cause of their quick return home.

"I can't believe Botular would do such a heinous thing! We must banish him from Sovorotskina immediately!" Queen Solinara expressed her outrage and disappointment.

"I understand, my love, why you feel this way. You feel as if Botular betrayed not only you but his own parents. But it is better to keep him here so we can watch him closely and monitor his thoughts. That way we will know if he is still trying to correspond with King Kaposkaran," Gateskin explained as he tried to calm his angry wife down.

"All right, Gateskin. You know what is best. I will keep a close watch over him and never let him out of my sight for a minute. I want him away from our children right now, though. We can build him a small cottage next to ours but far enough away to keep our children safe."

"I agree, Solinara. Please stay calm and don't let on you know about this message. We need to keep Botular in the dark about it for now. When it is necessary to share it with him, I will be the one to do so. I have plans to use it against him."

"Okay, Gateskin. I know you will take care of it. In the meantime, I have work to do to prepare some refreshments for our new citizens. Also, I will conjure up a Citizenship Certificates for each of them and an Adoption Certificate."

"Wonderful idea, Solinara. I don't know what I would do without you. You always think of everything I forget," Gateskin exclaimed. He reached forward and kissed his queen lightly on the lips as she passed by him. This gesture of affection brought a smile to her once angry countenance.

"Oh, Solinara, can you please conjure up a few medals for my new guards? I want to present them before the Adoption Ceremony."

"Of course, my love. It will be done." Solinara winked and smiled at her husband as she hurried back to the kitchen to work.

The King began the ceremony by asking all who were present, "Do you wish to be citizens of this great land of Sovorotskina?"

There was a loud chorus of 'ays' heard.

King Gateskin asked further, "Do you promise to be supportive of one another, assist your king and queen whenever requested, and always show kindness to each other and others in need?"

More 'ayes' were heard.

"Well, then I now pronounce that you are citizens of this fine Land of Sovorotskina!"

A symphony of cheering was heard that traveled all through the village. Even the village people a distance away could be heard cheering back in response.

After Gateskin performed the ceremony, he used Spindle to hand out the certificates. The eager Sprite stood on the high platform, specially made for him, so he could meet each new citizen of Sovorotskina in the eye.

Spindle was so excited to take part in this ceremony, that he didn't hear his name being called by the King, after he had handed out the last certificate.

King Gateskin had not had a Head Guard as such. He had always used several of his fellow Sovorotskinans to do guard duty, accompanying him on excursions or visits to the village. He knew it was time to have one and he had found the perfect person to fill the position. He turned toward Spindle.

"Spindle, are you prepared to become my Head Guard today?"

"What? What did you say, my King? Head Guard?"

"Yes, my good little man. I am proclaiming that you are to be my Head Guard, as of today."

Gateskin smiled upon the astonished face of Spindle, who was shaking all over, clearly in shock.

"I...I...I would be honored, good King Gateskin, to be your Head Guard. I am an unworthy subject. I only hope I will do you honor in my new position." Spindle bowed from his high perch to accept the medal and shook the King's hand.

Gateskin picked up the Sprite and put him on his shoulder to march around in display to all the new subjects. Spindle held his head up high as he showed off his new medal and waved at everyone. His proud parents waved back with beaming smiles. They had previously approved the King's choice just before the ceremony. Serena was watching on the sidelines. She waved and blew a kiss to Spindle who grabbed it in mid-air with a smile.

There was much clapping and rejoicing by all but the ceremony was not yet over.

Gateskin once again placed his new Head Guard, Spindle, on the raised platform to assist him in the next presentation. Gateskin gazed through the crowd of new citizens and he asked, "Who amongst you would like to become guards in this Land of Sovorotskina?"

Many hands were raised which made the King smile. He pointed out to Mitteran and several of other the men to come forward.

They were excited about this prospect and eagerly ran up to the stage. They waited for King Gateskin to give them further orders.

Addressing the men the King asked, "New citizens of Sovorotskina, are you willing to give your life to support and defend your new land?"

The men stood straight and tall and with pride they said in unison, "Yes, King Gateskin!"

"Then you shall be my new guards under the direction of me and my Head Guard, Spindle."

Spindle nearly fell off the platform in shock over the King's words. His face turned a beige color that was a form of blushing for a Sprite.

Each man was presented with a medal. Hands were shaken and backs were patted in congratulations as more cheers could be heard. The men settled back down in their seats when the King held up his hand for their attention.

"Now I am honored to perform this special presentation. "Hotenfaran, Procelina and Arubane, please come up to the stage for the Adoption Certification Presentation."

Hotenfaran took his wife's and soon-to-be son's hands and stepped onto the stage next to King Gateskin. Procelina's hands shook and her husband and Arubane squeezed her hands to calm her down. She looked at each of them and nodded with a wide smile and sparkling eyes.

Gateskin began, "We have a child, Arubane, here who is now a new citizen of Sovorotskina but is without parents. Do you Hotenfaran and Procelina promise to take care of Arubane, and always treat him with love and kindness?"

The Fairy and Wizard both answered loudly for all to hear, "Yes, we do!"

Gateskin looked down on Arubane and asked, "Arubane, do you promise to love, respect and be good to your new mother and father always?"

Arubane piped up in an excited voice, "Oh, yes I promise to always love, respect and honor them as my mother and father. I will also protect them from harm and be by their sides when they are old and need me there."

Procelina gasped at what her new son had said. She felt truly blessed to have such a wonderful little boy in their lonely lives. Their lives would be forever perfect from this day on.

Hotenfaran was speechless and tried not to show he was deeply moved to tears. He swiftly wiped away his tears with the back of his hand pretending to cough.

Procelina smiled at him and whispered, "It's okay, my love. I feel the same."

Gateskin announced proudly, "Well, now I pronounce you a family of three. Arubane, you can hug and kiss your mother and father now that you are officially their son."

Arubane flew up into the arms of his new mother and father and smothered them with hugs and kisses as tears flowed copiously from all three.

Hotenfaran held Arubane in his arms, not wanting to let go. He turned toward King Gateskin and grasped his hand tightly in his own and said, "Thank you, King Gateskin, for this beautiful ceremony. I can't tell you how much this means to me to now have a son. I will treasure him always."

"You are most welcome, Hotenfaran. You and Procelina deserve this beautiful child. You are long overdue for the happiness of being a family," King Gateskin responded with a smile and handed Hotenfaran the Adoption Certificate.

Hotenfaran grasped it in his hand and looked at it with a sigh. He nodded at the King and smiled through fresh tears.

Procelina stepped forward and hugged King Gateskin and whispered, "Thank you, dear King, for your kindness and thoughtfulness always."

"My pleasure, Procelina. Now let's celebrate in style. Here comes the refreshments created by my lovely wife."

Hearing this, Arubane jumped out of his father's arms and ran to get some food but not before turning back to again hug both parents fiercely.

The proud new parents watched their son as he sat at a table and helped himself to all kinds of goodies. Arubane talked excitedly with some of the new citizens and looked back from time to time to gaze at his adoring parents just to make sure they were still there and that this was not just a dream. They smiled and waved at him to ensure they were not going anywhere.

Procelina looked at Hotenfaran and said through tears of joy, "I have never been happier in my life other than when we first met. My life is now complete, my love. I have two people who are precious beyond belief to me."

"I feel the same, my beautiful wife. I feel the same." Hotenfaran hid the tears by hugging his wife closely so she wouldn't see them, again threatening to fall. After all, wizards are not supposed to cry.

Procelina hugged him back and smiled realizing what he needed to do – hide the tears for he was taught as a young child that boys don't cry. What he didn't realize is that real men often do and wizards too.

A NEW JOURNEY BEGINS

CHAPTER 58

Back at the castle of King Kaposkaran...

The four guards, after passing by the Gatekeeper's dead body at the square, arrived back at the castle to meet up with the ten other guards to lead them to the Cave in Crotesia Mountain. The guards realized now that they should not have come back to the Village. The sight of the Gatekeeper's dead body made the guards realize how truly cruel the King could be and this brought a deep fear to the surface which they were trying to keep contained. They dreaded this journey that could be the death of them all.

As their journey began, the guards heard this song reverberating throughout the trees of the forest. This song brought a chill to the guards' bones as the voices became louder and louder still.

From the Land of Darkness
To the Land of Light
We never let our enemies out of our sight.
As we travel high and travel low,
We always stay safe wherever we go.
May Faith & Love be with us each day.
May Magic & Mystery conjure up the words
we need to say.
May Peace & Harmony guide us on our way.
May Myths & Legends help us to stay strong,
we pray.

The guards continued on but shivered as they tried to drown out the sounds by covering their ears with their hands. The guards realized that size doesn't matter. When the Sprites worked together, they were formidable and feared. There would be no end to their powers. The four guards knew what this felt like on their previous journey but didn't share their experiences with the ten new guards. They were embarrassed to say that they felt intimidated by these little creatures who they could not see.

The other guards would find out soon enough what they were up against – the invisible enemy that was more powerful than they could ever imagine.

The adventure continues…

Not really   THE END

The adventure continues in Gateskin Chronicles Book 2.

Watch for Books 3-6 in the coming years.

ABOUT THE AUTHOR

Janice Spina is a retired administrative secretary from a public school system in Massachusetts. She has always loved writing poetry, novels and children's stories.

This is the 37th book Janice has published. She also has two mystery series of six books each, one for boys and the other for girls even though they both are enjoyed by either sex. She has published 18 children's stories for young children. She also writes under J.E. Spina and has published five novels and a short story collection for 18+.

She can be reached at these links.

Website: http://Jemsbooks.com
Twitter: http://twitter.com/janice_spina
FB Main Page:
http://facebook.com/janice.spina.9
FB Author Page:
http://facebook.com/janicespina7
FB Novelist Page:
http://facebook.com/jespina7
Blog: http://Jemsbooks.wordpress.com

Janice lives in New Hampshire with her husband, John, and two tanks of fish. John is the illustrator of her children's books and designer of all her book covers.

If you enjoyed this book, please leave a review where you purchased it and spread the word to your family and friends. Janice loves to hear from readers and welcomes reviews from wherever her books are purchased. She says, 'It's like Christmas each time I receive a review!'

If you would like to be on Janice Spina's email list to receive updates, newsletters, and special deals on books, please send a request to jjspina@comcast.net and put in subject line **JEMSBOOKS MAILING LIST**.

A NOTE FROM THE AUTHOR

This story was written over ten years ago. At that time, I wasn't ready to publish it. There were too many other books I wanted to publish first. I always enjoyed reading fantasy and wanted to create my own fantasy series for young adults.

This series is written for young adults – Ages 13-17, but can be enjoyed by adults too. I hope you enjoyed this work of fiction. Watch for more books in this series coming over the new few years.

Thank you for purchasing one of Jemsbooks. I appreciate your kind support of me and my books. If you like this book, a review would be greatly appreciated wherever you purchased it. Reviews and word of mouth are the best way to spread your thoughts about books. Please share your review with friends and family. I would love to hear from you. You can reach me at jjspina(at)comcast(dot)net.

All my books are available on Amazon and Barnes & Noble. Watch for more books coming for all ages.

With Blessings & Love,

Janice Spina

OTHER YA BOOKS BY JANICE SPINA

Middle-Grade/Preteen/Young Adult:

Davey & Derek Junior Detectives Book 1:
The Case of the Missing Cell Phone
   (Pinnacle Book Achievement Award,
   Honorable Mention- Readers'
Favorite Book Award)

Davey & Derek Junior Detectives Book 2:
The Case of the Mysterious Black Cat
   (Pinnacle Book Achievement Award)

Davey & Derek Junior Detectives Book 3: The Case of the Magical Ivory Elephant
   (Pinnacle Book Achievement Award &
Reader's

Favorite Book Awards – Silver Medal)

Davey & Derek Junior Detectives Book 4: The Case of the Brown Scraggly Dog
   (Finalist in Red City Review Awards & 5-Star Book Review – Readers' Favorite Book Awards)

Davey & Derek Junior Detectives Book 5:
The Case of the Sad Mischievous Ghost
   (Pinnacle Book Achievement Award & Authorsdb
   Cover Contest – Silver Medal)

Davey & Derek Junior Detectives Book 6: The Case of the Mystery of the Bells
   (Pinnacle Book Achievement Award, Finalist – Readers' Favorite Book Awards, Finalist – Book Excellence Awards)

Abby & Holly School Dance

(Pinnacle Book Achievement Award &
Bronze Medal from Readers' Favorite
Book Awards)

***Abby & Holly Series Book 2:
Unfortunate Events***
   (Pinnacle Book Achievement Award,
Readers' Favorite Book Awards –
Honorable Mention)

***Abby & Holly Series, Book 3, Secrets of
the Trunk***
   (Pinnacle Book Achievement Award)

***Abby & Holly Series, Book 4, The
Hidden Stairway***
   (Pinnacle Book Achievement Award)

***Abby & Holly Series, Book 5, The
Copper Key***
   (Pinnacle Book Achievement Award)

Abby & Holly Series, Book 6, Faulty Timeline

(Pinnacle Book Achievement Award)

BOOKS BY J.E. SPINA FOR 18+

Hunting Mariah (Finalist in Authorsdb First Lines Contest)

Mariah's Revenge (Finalist in Authorsdb First Lines Contest)

How Far is Heaven

An Angel Among Us: A Short Story Collection

In A Second

Lubelia Alycea: One Hundred Years